DEDICATION

This book is dedicated to my wife Davina Hepson who has supported me
in everything I have ever done and who has had the staying power to
suffer me all these years.

CONTENTS

ACKNOWLEDGMENTS

Thanks to all those 'Bad Boys' for supplying the inspiration for this book; however the story is purely fictional and is not based on any real person, place or situation.

CHAPTER 1   THE PECKING ORDER

I'm not going to claim that the following tale is a true story; however it is based around real people, events and circumstances. The names have been changed to protect the Guilty.

We pick it up on a cold Saturday morning in February nineteen ninety six. Colin Spears is waiting to start his second shift of a recently imposed Community Service Order. The previous week he had just kept his head down and his wits about him. The rules were simple enough, come here, do what your told, don't be late and any days off had better be covered by a Doctor's line, failure to comply would result in a prison sentence.

A little trickier was sussing out the other three guys who were unfortunate enough to be there with him. There was Brian something an alcoholic/junkie who looked so burnt out he was hard to put an age on. Brian had the privilege of going by two nicknames, Big Tam referred to him as 'The Creature' while in reference to how slowly he done anything, the Supervisor called him 'Rigor Mortis'. His brain was pretty much fried and he seemed harmless enough.

Then there was young Michael, seventeen, a wee boy full of big stories, he had been laying it on thick about how well known local nutter Chas Moncreif A.K.A. Monkey was his uncle. Colin had noticed from the tag on his overall that Mick's surname was Robertson;

'Heavy dude!' He commented.

Mick seemed to grow an inch taller. 'They all know better than to fuck with me.'

The work continued in silence for a full five minutes

'So Chas is your Dad's brother?'

'My dad's brother'.

Confirmed Mick blissfully unaware that he had just been sussed. Colin never cracked a light.

It was Big Tam McGuire, affectionately known as Mig that Colin was still trying to get a handle on. It had not occurred to Colin that he might find himself working alongside guys who had already done time. In Tams case; a couple of stints for serious assault. Probably the only reason he was doing community service was that it was the cheaper alternative. To be fair, so far he seemed okay; he was friendly enough and had a wicked sense of humour.

'Right get your arses in gear and get some paint on the walls...'

The Supervisor had spoken and it was time to start.

The painting begins, the Supervisor an ugly little man middle aged out of shape and balding sits in the corner reading The Daily Record, occasionally looking out from behind his paper with an authoritative.

'Get a move on.'

The pace of the work was slow and tedious, partly down to the fact that Colin and Mig were both hung over and partly because the walls they were painting had never been painted before. Consequently they were taking coat, after coat to little visible advantage, a phenomenon not lost on Colin.

'That's the third coat and the bricks are still shining through.'

The big man's pissed off expression was reply enough.

'Half-past-ten, and since I'm in a good mood you can have ten minutes for a smoke.'

'Since I'm in a good mood.' Mimicked Colin.

'Benevolent Bastard.'

Colin and Mig sat on upturned paint tins, Mig gestured with his Tobacco tin.

'Would you like a Roll Up?'

'No you're alright.'

He produced a packet of Regal and lit up.

'So have you been up to anything exciting since last week.'

'A Mate in the trade put in an order for an RS Turbo. It took me a few days to locate one that wasn't kept overnight in a locked garage but I got it sorted on Thursday night and passed it on to him. A quick five hundred in hand and everybody's happy.'

Young Michael, who had a big problem when it came to minding his own business suddenly appeared and asked excitedly.

'Are they going to ring it?'

Mig looked slightly taken aback.

'Ring it... get yourself to fuck. The screws are well wide to that one these days. No by now it will have been broken for parts, an engine here, and a gearbox there, a nice set of alloy's somewhere else.'

'How did you get passed the alarm?'

'I broke the front left indicator, removed the bulb, ran a wire from the socket to the body and bumped the car, setting off the alarm, the first flash of the hazards shorted out the fuse. The alarm and door seen to, we pushed it well away from the drive before we started it.'

Michael listened intently.

'Check the Wee Mans face, he just learned something.'

'What if the guy had come out?'

'Don't you worry Wee Man, we had it covered.'

He was starting to tire of Michael's curiosity.

'How... how did you have it covered?'

Colin could see the change in Mig's body language.

'We had one of the boys sitting outside his front door with a three-foot piece of Scaffolding pole. You try running after somebody, with a broken leg.'

The change in his tone was lost on Mick the Mouth, who, before Colin had a chance to say something diplomatic asked.

'Who did you sell it to?'

Mig was about to discuss the virtue of minding your own business, when, fortunately for the Mouth he had noticed that the Supervisor, although out of earshot, was currently looking in their direction. Colin attempted to defuse the situation.

'There are some things that you just don't ask.'

The Supervisor approached.

'What about getting those walls painted, you didn't get off with the Jail just so you could sit about smoking fags and chatting each other up in my time.'

Reluctantly they got back to work. Colin and Mig worked side by side. It was Colin who spoke first.

'That Bastard has an attitude problem.'

Mig put on his best posh voice.

'I disagree with your diagnosis Dr Spears, and would offer a second opinion. I believe that the Supervisor's affliction runs much, much deeper than just the obvious problem with his attitude. Having studied his symptoms closely over several weeks, I am convinced beyond all doubt that he is in the advanced stages of a condition that we in the profession refer to as, being a Total Fanny.'

This made Colin laugh. Mig continued in a serious tone

'I note your concern. But the situation is not without some hope, this condition has been successfully treated in the past.'

He paused for a moment.

'Therefore I am prescribing a swift kick in the Ghoulies, to be administered three times a day. However should unthinkable happen and the symptoms persist, he is to be kicked in the Ghoulies five times a day, until such times as a full recovery is made.'

Colin was helpless with laughter as was Mick this even got a reaction out of Rigor Mortis attracting the attention of the Supervisor.

'Something you'd like to say to me boys.......?'

No one said anything.

'No I didn't think so....'

He laughed sarcastically as he turned and headed towards his chair — Mig wasn't about to let it go and muttered under his breath.

'You're a wee ugly Prick....'

'What did you call me...?'

'I never called you anything.'

'You called me a Prick.'

'You heard me Colin, what I said was, the paints not very thick.'

Mig wore his best Innocent expression.

'Can you see what I'm up against here, the man's trying to bend my words just to get me in to trouble?'

'Get on with it, just get on with it the jails aren't that full that they couldn't find a few more places for you lot.'

'Calm down now Boys, we don't want to find ourselves breached, and up in front of a Judge on that most serious charge of commenting on how thick the paint is while carrying out our community service.'

'Just get those walls done.'

He retreated back to his seat and his paper to Mig's parting shot of.

'But the paints not very thick.'

Again the painting resumes.

'You rattled his Cage.'

'Maybe in future he'll stick to hiding behind his paper.'

'Does it not worry you that he might breach you.'

The big man smiled. 'I've done more porridge than the three Bears —

empty threats of the Nick do not impress me.'

It was long, cold and tedious and it seemed that wee Mick was repeating…

'What time is it now, it's dragging in...'

Every five minutes on the five minutes. Colin actually feared he would snap and seriously assault him with an emulsion soaked paint brush, but finally it was dinner time and everyone sat around eating their various pieces. It was at this point that Mig turned his attention to young Michael.

'So Wee Man, how did you get to be here?'

Michael was naïve enough to be flattered by this attention.

'I stole a Motor...'

No one seemed that impressed. Undeterred by this he continued.

'It was a Honda Prelude... 2.2, sixteen valves.'

It had in fact been a beaten up old Fiesta with a blowing exhaust.

'The police were chasing me in a 5 series BMW.'

Mick the Mouth was starting to get into his swing.

'You should have seen it, a hundred mile an hour along those twisty wee back roads. Their bottle must have gone because I lost the pursuit Car.'

This was the disturbing thing about the Mouth; it was almost as though he believed his own stories.

'So there I am cruising along at a ton wondering what my Mammy has on for the tea, when I hear the chopper coming.'

Mig subtly winks at Colin.

'There's not much you're going to do about that Wee Man.'

'Tell me about it.'

Mick's imagination had moved into Warp Drive.

'So it was time to do a runner, a ditched the motor in a field, next thing I know the police are everywhere. I managed to batter a couple of them then about seven of them all jumped me at the same time.'

Wearing his best dead pan expression.

'So how much time did you get Wee Man?'

'I never got time. I got eighty hours Community Service.'

'You never got time... Let's think about this; you took and drove away, you obviously have no license, you were involved in a high speed chase, they had to bring out the chopper. Add to that resisting arrest and two counts of police assault...' Mig paused for best effect.

'And all you got was eighty hours Community Service?'

'I got a hundred-and-fifty pound fine as well'

Added Wee Mick rapidly.

Colin and Mig start to laugh, Michael was starting to lose his cool and he wasn't about to let be let off the hook.

'Either your Mammy was sleeping with the judge or you'll need to give me the name of your brief.'

Colin couldn't resist it.

'I've heard of his brief. He's a guy called Jesus. Just call Nazareth 90210.'

The laughter continued, the big man decided to change tack.

'No, but seriously.... I take it that you have stolen a few cars in your time.'

'Hundreds' Lied Mick, unconvincingly.

'Hundreds you say, but you obviously don't know how to get round an alarm... And if you don't know how to get round an alarm... I'd be very interested to know how you managed to hoist the motor you were telling us about.'

Michael was so flustered that he blurts out the truth.

'The guy had left the keys in it.'

More laughter, wee Mick's face is bright red, he is almost in tears.

'Check it out Colin, you could fry eggs on that face.'

'Fuck off the lot of you... I'm away for a piss.'

Colin's turn. 'Houston we have a problem... The Lunar Michael has veered off course and is heading at great speed towards the Lavvy...'

The toilet door slams shut.

'The Lunar Michael has crashed — all credibility has sunk without trace.'

The Supervisor gets to his feet.

'What's going on over there?'

'It's just Wee Mick'

Replied Mig. 'He's having a character building experience.'

A few moments later, Brian something AKA the creature AKA rigor mortise followed Michael to the toilet.

'That looks a bit suss.' Commented Mig.

'He's probably going to check that the wee man's not decided to end it all by drowning himself down the S bend.'

'So the Creature, what's his story?'

'Well according to wee Mick.'

'No don't tell me, let me guess... He's wee Mick's uncle and he got his community service for urinating in a public place, but he's really an axe murdering Cannibal.'

'He told the wee man that the police picked him up lying

unconscious outside Flanagan's bar one Wednesday afternoon, he remembers it was a Wednesday because that's the day he got his Giro.'

The big man found this amusing.

'The police, they're alright that way, adds a whole new meaning to the expression lifted.'

'The police — where would we be without them'

'The police are one thing, Mr Morgan, he was something else.

'Who's he?'

'Morgan was Chief Turnkey down in Durham, Morgan the Organ we called him. Loved his Job, hated the Scots and I was the only Jock on that Wing.'

'You get them.'

'Morgan maintained that if he ran things — the Bastards would be locked in twenty-four-seven, bread and water, but only for good behaviour and electric shocks every hour on the hour.'

Colin burst out laughing.

'It's alright laughing but the Bastard was serious... I might have wound up the boy, but at least I didn't go plugging him into the mains.... no compared to some, I'm your actual Humanitarian.'

The Supervisor headed for the toilet. Mig noticed his cigarettes left by his chair, he's on them the second the toilet door closes He removed four of the remaining seventeen cigarettes before replacing the packet to its previous position, lighter on top as before. He offers them to Colin.

'Here, regal same as yours, stick them in your packet quick.'

Colin starts to panic. 'Risk the Jail for four fags? I don't think so.'

Grinning from ear to ear.

'They're the same as yours, how could he prove it, you have about three seconds until he comes back out of there.'

No sooner than the fags were stashed, the door opened, out comes the Mouth and the Creature followed by the Supervisor, who was in good voice.

'If I get any more skiving I will be taking it up with the office.'

Mig couldn't resist it.

'Surely we have time for another Fag.'

Colin cringed; the Supervisor totally ignored the question.

'It's bad for you anyway'

Continues to ignore him.

'We should all be trying to cut down.'

'Less of it McGuire, the lot of you get back to work.'

The painting of the thankless walls resumes, it is Mig who speaks first.

'Would you like me to tell you how I seen my own of Morgan the Organ.'

The curiosity in Colin's face was answer enough.

'It will make a good story for the Pub. That's assuming you fancy a pint after the shift.'

The big man would not have been Colin's first choice of someone to go for a pint with. He was unpredictable enough when sober but the sharp wit and sense of humour coupled with the curiosity of how he could put one over on a prison guard had won him over.

'I drink in the Wee Barrel.'

'That's Monkey's watering hole.'

'Moncreif's a nut job; I just keep out of his way. We could make it somewhere else.'

Mig had a reputation to think of.

'The Wee Barrel will do for me. I've heard it's a good pint in there.'

The rest of the shift went without incident apart from the Supervisor counting his fags and scratching his head.

CHAPTER 2   IT WASN'T WHAT I THOUGHT IT WAS

It was as they left the factory unit Mig gestured to the Factory black, Ford Capri 2.8 injection that Colin had admired the week before.

'This is my Machine'

'It looks minted'

'I try to look after it. It's a 1986, not bad for a twelve year old car. It was one of the last Capri's off the production line. When I was a kid, I was a big fan of the TV show 'The Professionals''

'Ah, right — Bodie and Doyle!'

'I always wanted a 2.8 — jump in!'

Colin sat in the passenger seat; it was so low it was almost like sitting on the floor. The Engine roared in to life at the first turn of the key. As the revs grew Colin felt a mixture of fear and excitement.

'It sounds pretty lively'

Mig grinned. 'That's what one hundred and sixty horsepower sounds like'

There was a sudden scream of protest from the back wheels and he was pinned to the seat as Mig changed up the gears. The landscape flew by at an increasingly alarming rate. After what seemed a very long time they scream to a halt outside the Wee Barrel. Much to Colin's relief he is still alive and uninjured. When they get out of the car Mig looked back at his pride and joy.

'The Capri always was a bit slippy on the back end.'

A handling flaw not lost on Colin on the ten minute white-knuckle ride to the Pub.

'But you can't really argue with that sort of straight line acceleration.'

Colin wasn't about to argue, his knee's were shaking and he wasn't even sure he was capable of speech.

'It has it all; the starfish alloy's, the rear spoiler, the, the half leather interior.'

He had slightly recovered.

'The on-board psychopath.'

Mig was still laughing as they entered the pub to the sound of 'MMM Bop' by Manson blaring from the juke box. They made their way to the bar.

'Have you seen the wee guys that sing that?'

'They're about ages with your Capri. Good song though'

'My shout, what are you having?'

'A pint of lager, to get the taste of the paint out of my throat.'

Mig looked around him.

'It's been maybe four or five years since I was last in here, new carpet fresh wallpaper but still the same old place. I'm even sure that guy sitting at the end of the bar was wearing that same jumper.'

The barmaid approached to take their order. Mig's attention was immediately drawn to the pretty face and long black hair that hung down her neck to a low top revealing a more than ample cleavage.

'Not that there hasn't been some improvements, two lager please!'

The pints were poured and paid for.

'Are you sure you don't want a half to go with that.'

'No a pint's fine.'

They took up their drinks and moved to a nearby table. The pub was reasonably busy for the last gasp of a Saturday afternoon.

'Your Capri — how long have you had it?'

'Must be nearly three years.'

'I'll bet it wasn't cheap.'

'I have a mate in the trade Martin he does damaged repairable's. Well that's his front all sorts of stuff finds it's way in and out of that garage. I bought the Capri as a cat C write off'

'What does that mean?'

'Cat C means the car is not beyond repair but it's cheaper for the insurance to write it off than to fix it. In the case of the Capri the previous owner had wrapped it round a pole.'

'You would never know it looking at it.'

'Martin's good at what he does. I gave him so much up front and acquired a few cars for him everybody's happy.'

Linda passed by rounding up empty glasses.

'I wouldn't mind getting to know her better.'

'That's Linda — she's a friend of Marion's and you are not alone, many have tried.'

'I like a challenge.'

'Anyway you were going to tell me how you seen your own of Morgan the Organ.'

He smiled; this was a memory that pleased him. He swallowed some of his pint then spoke.

'Morgan was the type of bastard that would see you mopping the floor, kick over your bucket then give you a lecture because of the mess and give it — don't argue with me McGuire. At lock up he would slam your shutter as loud as he could, then it was the handle to the door, bang, just to rub it in that that was you dubbed up for the night.'

'Sounds like a proper little Hitler.'

'Tried his best, anyway, it was my last night, I was getting released the following morning. Just as luck would have it Morgan was on lock up.'

Paused for a moment to drink from his pint.

'I could hear him coming, bang, banging his way down the corridor. He got to my cell and looked in the shutter, and there I was all cosy up on the top bunk checking out the reader's wives section of my favourite magazine. I said 'good night Mr Morgan, remember and look me up first time your in Scotland.' He just glared; bang went the shutter, bang went the handle, then onto the next cell bang, bang, then onto the next cell then, oh dear only one bang followed by an angry scream, as all too soon the Organ discovered that the handle to that cell was all covered in shite.'

The punch-line had been perfectly timed Colin almost choked on the mouthful of lager that he was in the process of drinking. He had lost count of how many times the big man had made him laugh in the last few hours. After composing himself he went to the bar to order a second round.

Mig watched as Linda collected the empty glasses. To a guy like him, the combination of black nylon and a tight black mini-skirt was a treat not to be missed. Colin returned with the pints.

'What did you get your CS hours for?'

He mimicked wee Mick's voice. 'I stole a Motor.....'

They both laughed.

'Seriously though?'

'I used to work for Matrix Electronics.'

'The place out near the bridge?'

'That's the one. Anyway over a few months I managed to liberate a sizable amount of computer chips and made rather a lot of money, thank you very much.'

The big man seemed impressed and raised his glass.

'A good score and no time served, I'll drink to that.'

'What they managed to pin on me was a drop in the Ocean as to what I actually took them for.'

'Even better!'

'I had already accepted that I was going down for it, my main concern was for how long. When the Judge said two-hundred and forty hours Community Service I felt as though I had just won the lottery.'

'I'll bet you had a few pints that night.'

'And then some.'

What he had omitted to say was that immediately after leaving the Court he ran to the nearest toilet and threw his guts up.

'I think what really swung it was that I had a decent lawyer and no previous.'

'No previous!'

Repeated Mig, almost in disbelief.

'Look I'm not going to insult your intelligence, It's not like I haven't pulled a few manoeuvres in my time, I just always knew how far to push it.'

He lifted his pint and quickly downed a couple of mouthfuls, then continued.

'I was always smart enough not to get caught I made it to twenty six without having a record, not bad eh.'

'Until this time?' enquired Mig

'I never got caught this time either.'

His mood became serious.

'Well not fair and square anyway. They knew it was me that was stealing the chips but they just couldn't work out how I was doing it. It got so bad towards the end that they were stopping and searching me just about every night, they kept switching the security as well. I think they thought the security were in on it.'

'Were they?'

'No they were just stupid. In the end they had one of the guards claim that he had caught me with chips on me.'

'The bastards fitted you up.'

I suppose they felt they could justify it. The Guard that done it was called Gordon McPhee.'

Mig recognised the name.

'Big guy, about six-foot-two, ages with me?'

'That's him.'

'I know him. The bastard went to the same School as me.'

He drained his pint… 'And I know where he lives.'

'Don't worry....'

Colin could still visualise McPhee lying through his teeth while giving evidence against him. 'So do I! ...'

'When you decide to look this guy up, give me a shout.'

This was a breath of fresh air, he had a strong urge for revenge but any time he mentioned it Marion always the voice of reason would say leave it alone, quit while you are ahead, we don't need any more trouble.

'I appreciate that. It's just a wee bit soon after the event, if you know what I mean.'

'Any time you like.' Getting to his feet he lifted the empty glasses.

'I'll get them in and when I get back you can tell me how you were getting the chips out.'

'You're on.'

He returned about ten minutes later pints in hand.

'You took your time, let me guess you were trying to charm your way into wee Linda's knickers.'

Mig placed the pints on the table and sat down.

'I was making progress. Anyway you were going to tell me how you were getting the chips out.'
Colin grinned; it still amused him that they never worked it out.

'First they would run the scanner over you, and then they would frisk you.'

'Sounds thorough enough to me. So how did you get round it?'

'The best ideas are the simplest ones. What happens if you run one of those scanners over, say, a metal belt buckle, or a steel toe cap boot?'

'It goes off and no one thinks anything of it.'

Mig was impressed.

'Nice one, you had the chips hidden in your boots. Fuck sake imagine the security not sussing that one.'

'Matrix paid their security national minimum wage, for that kind of money a brain's not usually included.'

Colin was enjoying himself; it was turning out to be not a bad day. Just at that he noticed Chas Moncreif enter the pub, as usual, flanked by his two sidekicks Hodgey and Dodgey. Space suddenly appeared at the bar; they ordered a round then started glaring over in Mig's direction. Colin was about to mention this.

'It's cool, I don't miss anything, if the cunt comes over, leave the talking to me.'

It didn't take long. Moncreif walked over and got right in Mig's face.

'I think it's about time you were leaving.'

The expression was dead pan.

'I'll leave this pub when I am ready and not before.'

This was not the answer that Moncreif wanted. He glared more intently;

the rest of the pub had fallen quiet, adding to the tension.

'I'm trying to enjoy a pint here, so either make your move or get out of my face.'

To the surprise of a lot of people not least Colin, Moncreif walked back over to the bar.
'I've never seen him back off from anybody before.'

Mig figured it wasn't over and changed the subject.

'This security Guard when would you like to look him up.'

This was not something that he wanted to get into. He pointed to the half empty glass, a half pint to top that up he suggested. Mig nodded and he made his way to the bar. Wee Linda's top looked tighter than ever, Moncreif looked uglier than ever.

'Your mate's getting it.'

Colin could not think of an appropriate reply. He lifted the drinks and turned to walk.

'You'll be lucky if I don't do you as well you prick.'

He returned with the drinks as he sat down the big man got up.

'I'll be back in a minute.'

Entering the Gents toilets. It was as he remembered it, about fifteen feet long by six feet wide. He stood with his back to the far wall — to the right the urinals to the left the sinks. He wasn't disappointed, Moncreif and Co were right behind him.

'Watch the door!' Ordered Moncreif.

The two gleeful grinning faces were more than happy to stand at his back. Moncreif and Mig sized each other up; Moncreif stood around six foot two weighing something over sixteen stone. Mig was about an inch smaller, at twenty five around five years younger and with an unhealthy appetite for amphetamines, stood a lean thirteen stone. Mig put his right hand up and asked..

'Before we start this, just what's your problem?'

'What's my problem! You're the bastard that slashed my nephew.'

Mig looked momentarily confused. Moncreif believed he was in total control and was going to enjoy the moment.'

'Wee Willie Moncreif, anorexic looking skinhead, small head, big ears also known as Wing Nut.'

'He was into one of my mates to the tune of nine hundred quid.'

'Don't talk shite; nobody would lend him that sort of money.'

'He wasn't loaned money, he was given substances on the understanding sale or return. He didn't sell them and he sure as fuck didn't return them, do you get the picture.'

'So you admit it then.'

Moncreif took a step forwards, he was now less than two feet away.

Mig raised his two hands out in front of him palms out in an apologetic manner.

'Look Chas I'm not looking for any...'

Moncreif was still waiting to hear the word trouble, when the head butt landed breaking his nose and rendering him semi-conscious. He was thrown against the sinks, the back of his head smashing the mirror above. He was then slammed head first into the opposite wall sliding face first down into the urinal.

The attack had been so calculated and savagely executed it had only taken seconds; the grins were gone from the faces, replaced by fear and disbelief. It was about to get a whole lot worse. Mig suddenly produced an eight inch lock back, his face was showing all the compassion and mercy you might expect from a rabid dog. The invitation was a simple one...

'Let's go!'

Colin was almost knocked to the ground, his attempt to enter the toilet, coinciding with the frenzied stampede to leave it. Hodgey and Dodgey had cleared the pub doors in the time it took to blink. Entering on his second attempt he was horrified to see Mig standing, knife in hand and Moncreif lying motionless on the floor.

'For fuck sake, what have you done?'

'I never stabbed him if that's what you think.'

Mig folded the knife and put it back into his pocket.

'Let's get to fuck before the Screws turn up.'

Mig walked through the pub ten foot tall with Colin tagging behind him, as the rest of the punters looked on in silent disbelief.

'What was it about?'

'Funnily enough, not what I thought it was. It seems I had a run in with his nephew.'

'How what did you think it was?'

'I thought he had found out I had been shagging his wife.'

CHAPTER 3   IN A SLUM NOT TOO FAR AWAY

Thursday night stopping time Colin makes his way through the Factory to clock out, the poisonous waft of burning plastic from the shrink wrapping machine caught his breath and hastened his pace. Just one more thing to add to the long list of reasons that he hated the place. The work was tedious and low paid and there was the usual mix of smarmy self important Management in the office and on the shop floor aggressive Hairies continually in each others faces; usually underpinned by the good old Celtic Rangers sectarian thing. He had been there six months now. He took the job mainly because his trial had been coming up.

Passing the loading bay he encountered McKenzie who was sitting on his forklift cursing a late order that had come in as this was going to add at least an hour onto his working day. McKenzie was your typical factory forklift driver, wanting to go everywhere at full speed, preferably round corners in reverse. In his first week in the job he had almost been run over by the forklift, an incident that had almost come to blows at the time and had over the months, deteriorated into an ongoing slanging match. Colin's nickname for McKenzie was Mad Mac and he had used a black ink marker to draw a pair of eyes on the front of his forklift.

'It's alright for some.' Shouted Mad Mac

Colin could not hide the smug expression.

'I'll think about you when I'm in the Pub downing my first pint.'

'I'll think about you when I'm counting my wages...'

'Never you mind thinking about wages, you just concentrate on what you're doing, that way there will be no fatalities.'

Mad Mac replied to this by aggressively revving the forklift a few times.

'I can taste the pint already.'

Wit failing him, the disgruntled McKenzie opted for the two finger salute. Colin mimicked taking a drink from a pint and walked away laughing. He was in a good mood, it was Thursday the wages were in the bank and as was his usual custom he would drop in to the local for a couple before going home. Hopefully after the incident on Saturday he wouldn't be barred. Short of being with Mig he hadn't actually done anything.

As he entered the pub he saw Hodgey and Dodgey standing at the bar. The upside to this was there were only two pints in front of them suggesting that Moncreif was not with them. The jukebox was belting out Chumbawumba's 'Tub Thumping' He took up position on the opposite end of the bar, his back was to the pool table. The table was not being used and there was a pool cue within easy reach. He ordered a pint, it was poured and brought to him, he pulled a fiver from his wallet.

Linda informed him. 'It's already been paid for.'

She gestured to Hodgey and Dodgey who were looking over. He looked back at them. 'Cheers!'

'Nae bother!' Was the overly friendly reply.

Colin was puzzled. Linda looked like she wanted to talk.

'Will your big pal be in tonight?'

'I wouldn't think so; I kind of figured he would have been barred.'

She winked at him.

Her voice was hushed and firm. 'Nobody in here saw anything.'

'Between you and me, there was more than a few folk in here happy to see that big bastard get it.'

Colin lowered his voice.

'What about Statler and Waldorf over there, what are they saying about it.'

'Very little, they near had a panic attack when they saw you come in, I think they're scared the big man's looking for them.'

'Their fears could be well founded and that would explain them buying me a pint, it's not like I know them.'

'What's his name?'

There was a twinkle in her eye.

'Tam McGuire but he generally goes by Mig, I'll tell him you were asking for him.'

Hodgey and Dodgey had lifted their pints and had come round to his side of the bar; he turned to face them it was Dodgey who spoke.

'Mind if we join you.'

Time to play it by ear, he gestured to a nearby table.

'Let's grab a seat!'

First things first, get the awkward question out of the way.

'Where's Chas the night?'

There was a sudden tension in the air; again it was Dodgey who spoke.

'He's still in the General.'

Colin suddenly felt uncomfortable.

''I didn't realise he was that badly hurt, I thought it was just his nose.'

Dodgey cringed as he re lived the memory.

'It was a lot worse than that. Mig bounced his head off of the walls a couple of times; he had a fractured skull and concussion.'

'The Doctors were pretty worried there were all sorts of CAT scans.'

Concern was starting to grow. 'How is he now?'

'His face is all bruised to fuck. But he seems okay, they're just holding onto him for a few days for observation. Funny thing is he has absolutely no recollection of going into the toilet.'

Colin could feel himself starting to break into a sweat.

'Were the police involved?'

'They were up at the hospital looking for a statement and when Chas told them that he couldn't remember they accused him of taking the piss.'

Dodgey drank from his pint before carrying on.

'This was a bit ironic, because it's probably the first time in his whole life that he actually told the truth to the police. Anyway you know the police, Chas gets into fights on a weekly basis this time he was the one that came off second best, like they actually care.'

This last comment was music to his ears, the police weren't interested, Moncreif had been reigning bully in that pub for long enough, the bastard had had it coming and the fact that it was his new found big mate, who had done it, was just the icing on the cake, and there was still one question to be asked.

'So do they reckon there's brain damage?'

'We were up yesterday; he was sitting up in bed chatting up the nurses and growling about the food, seems normal to us.'

'Mind you we figured the big cunt for brain damage in the first place.'

Chipped in Hodgey to the amusement of all, Colin checked his watch.

'Back in a minute!'

He made his way to the pay phone and called home, the call was answered on the second ring.

'Hi love it's me, I'm in the Wee Barrel.'

'Of course you are, where else would you be at this time on a Thursday?'

She was scolding in a light-hearted manner.'

'And I suppose your going to tell me that you'll be home in half an hour.'

'I'll be about half an hour.'

'Colin, it's me you're talking to and we both know that you will be at least an hour.'

'Okay. I'll be about an hour; I'll bring you back a wee quarter bottle.'

'Don't be any longer than an hour, I got some news today that I am dying to tell you about.'

'Can you not tell me now?'

'No!'

'Why not?'

'Never mind why not, when you get home, don't be long, bye.'

As the phone went down his curiosity went up, he had heard that happy mirthful tone before funnily enough on that same phone on another Thursday night. On that occasion he had went home to the living room walls half stripped and the new paper and paste sitting in the middle of the floor, his wife had a sense of humour.

Marion sat on the floor next to the phone; she picked it up on the first ring.

'I'm not telling you till you get home; we are having Kippers for tea, mind now an hour, no longer.'

She put the phone down. He was dumbfounded she had known the two things he was going to ask in the order he was going to ask them and managed to get a dig in about how long he should be. He hadn't even managed to get a word off. The woman was impossible. He could picture her sitting by the phone laughing; she had been laughing a lot since the trial. Other than the uncertainty of the trial and the length of time it had dragged out the last couple of years had been good to them, he had managed to clear off the rent arrears, all be it with stolen money and the council had given them their own back and front door. They had done the place up like a palace. The bills were a little behind but that was just to put a look on things, in reality no one could touch them.

When they had redecorated the bedroom he had cut out and replaced a square foot of plasterboard on the back wall before papering over it, in there he had put the rainy day money, just a little under ten thousand pounds.

He returned to his seat.

'When will you see Mig?' Inquired Dodgey nervously.

33

'We do community service together. I'll see him on Saturday.'

'Could you tell him that me and Hodgey, we weren't really into that on Saturday?'

'No we were the ones trying to talk Chas out of it.'

Added Hodgey unconvincingly. Colin struggled hard not to laugh.

'It's not like we were going to do anything, it's just we hang around with Chas and we were kind of expected to be there, if you know what I mean.'

He figured it best to humour them.

'I'll mention that when I see him, he can be quite reasonable sometimes.'

'Another pint?' Offered Dodgey.

This was a tempting offer but curiosity was starting to bite.

'Would have liked one, but I promised the missus I would only stay for the one. I'll see you around!'

As he made to leave the pub he was shouted back by Linda.

'Hold on a minute.'

She handed Colin a small piece of paper.

'Here's my number. Tell Mig if he still wants a date to give me a call.'

As he took the number from her hand he couldn't help noticing the shimmering black nylon pulled tight over shapely thighs, barely hidden at all, under the shortest of skirts and thought to himself 'lucky bastard.'

'I'll give it to him when I see him on Saturday.'

Even as they spoke — in a slum not too far away the Capri pulled to a halt. Here it was the Scheme, the run down cancerous under belly of suburbia a no-man's-land of blown about rubbish and roaming under-fed dogs. A whole street perfectly lit by streetlights, six rows of tenements all with doors and windows boarded up, every one with the full metal jacket. Every one except for the immediate bottom right, the one with the Spice Girls music blaring from the open window, and the Cosworth Sierra sitting outside. If this wasn't the Twilight Zone it came pretty fucking close. Mig admired the car on his way to the close reflecting, nice motor shame about the tacky racing stripe but then Andy Gallagher occupier of this unusual residence, owner of that particular car, never did have any class, money, yes, in abundance, he was the local drug baron. Class? Well, despite making thousands a week, he still had the audacity to have his electricity meter rigged. Mig chapped the letterbox, the gruff voice from behind the door demanded.

'Who is it?
'It's me... Mig.'

Various locks and deadbolts were undone before the door opened a few inches. Gallagher looked out to confirm it actually was Mig before removing the final chain.

'Where are the dogs?'

His two Staffies Ronnie and Reggie, were vicious little bastards, they didn't actually bark, they would just fly out and try to remove your legs. Mig didn't want a repeat of his last visit.

'You're okay, they're in the room.'

'You have this place better dubbed up than some of the cells I've been in.'

'In my line of business, you never know who might come to your door.'

The living room was freshly decorated with up lighters around the walls. The pine floorboards were highly polished; there was a white leather suite so new you could still smell the hide. Sitting on the settee was a girl of about eighteen or nineteen by the way she was dressed she was obviously on the game. As they entered the room she lowered her head as though she was shy, closer inspection revealed that she had a black eye. Gallagher gestured to one of the chairs.

'Park your arse.'

'Mig this is Suzy. Suzy this is Mig, he's a mate of mine.'

35

The girl said nothing as though unsure of what to say. Gallagher got annoyed.

'Hoi, shit for brains! I said the guy's a friend. So get your skinny wee arse through to the kitchen and bring back a couple of beers and on your way out you can turn that fucking noise off. For the first time today I've had the chance of some intelligent conversation.'

The girl pulled the door shut as she left the room.

'Who's she?'

His voice was raised good and loud.

'She's no anybody; she is just some wee junkie slapper that's keeping my bed warm for a couple of nights.'

The girl re-entered the room, looking like she might have cried had she not already had all feeling beaten out of her. Mig pretended to be unaffected by this. The cans were placed on the coffee table.

'Now get yourself to fuck, there's business to be discussed.'

Head down she left the room.

'What do you think of the suite, got it two weeks ago, three-and-a-half-grand from that place down the industrial estate?'

'Nice suite, but you should have asked for a discount, on account of the fag burns on the arms.'

Gallagher laughed and handed Mig an envelope.

'For services rendered.'

A quick look inside revealed there to be one hundred pounds, this did not please Mig.

'The deal was two hundred; I held up my end, the guy got chibbed.'

'I'll give you the other hundred on the recovery of the debt.'

The change in tone had caused Ronnie and Reggie to start barking, adding to the tension.

'I know for a fact that when Wing Nut got marked up a lot of the tick that was owed to you came in. So before you give me any more shite I'll have the other hundred just now. If you don't mind.'

The smile on his face did little to hide the anger in his voice.

'Okay... You can have the other hundred just now.'

Suddenly he produced a wad that would actually have choked a horse, laughing again, as he counted off one hundred pounds. This annoyed Mig even more.

'While we are talking business, I was planning to do a bit of dealing myself.'

Gallagher did not look the slightest bit amused at this revelation.

'Nothing fancy, just a wee bit of blow here and there, maybe the odd Ecky now and again.'

There was some serious eye contact before Gallagher caved in.

'Okay. On two conditions, you don't use my supplier you find your own and no coke or smack, that's my market.'

'Fair enough, I thought it was only right to give you your place and tell you first.'

'Would you like another beer?'

Having no desire to see the girl humiliated again Mig declined the offer.

'No, I have to go, I have something else to attend to. In the unlikely event you don't get squared up the minute he gets his criminal injures; I'll mark up the other side of his face and give you your money back.'

CHAPTER 4   DON'T THINK OF IT AS BREAKING THE LAW

Saturday morning again, last nights snow had turned to slush and if it was possible it felt colder inside than out.

'Brass monkeys stay in on days like this.' Commented Colin.

The big man stamped his feet and rubbed his hands together.

'I'm not saying it's cold but it's starting to get pretty testy around my frosticles. There must be a law against making us work in these temperatures.'

Mick stood grumbling about the absence of a heater. The Creature looked dazed from the night before and just stared into space. The Supervisor was in good form.

'Oh you wee souls, my heart bleeds for you. I have an idea McGuire why don't you go back and tell the Judge that it's too cold to work and see what he says.'

'Does that mean we can go home?'

'You can go home if you want McGuire. I'll just put you down as a failed to attend and with a bit of luck I will never see you again.'

The hint of going to prison was not lost on Colin.

'I suppose if we don't want to freeze to death where we are standing we had better start working.'

He was hung over and unfortunately found himself working next to Mick the mouth who was talking non stop for what seemed like a long time — going on and on about the Spice girls and what he would like to do with them.

Ten-thirty it was time for a smoke break. Hardly had they lit up when a tremendous smell hit the air, a stench of such hideous proportions that no one was about to own up to it.

'For fuck sake...'

Commented Mig holding his nose and taking a couple of steps back.

Colin figured it had been Mick the mouth who had let rip. Releasing this foulest of odours.

'Listen wee man I know we were winding you up last week but there was no need to take your revenge in such a dire manner.'

Michael fearing this was the start of the day to come went red in the face.

'It wasn't me, I bet it was him.'

He blurted pointing to Rigor Mortis, who replied with a non committal.

'I'm saying nothing.'

'No change there then.' Got in Mig.

Colin produced the piece of paper Linda had given him.

'Linda the barmaid asked me to give you her phone number. She said to phone her if you still want to go out on a date.'

Mig placed the piece of paper in his back pocket.

'You don't seem too surprised.'

'Why would I be surprised, she's seen me once? She's probably read about me as well.'

'Read about you?' Echoed young Michael.

'In the Barmaids weekly. Rampant sex machine McGuire for hire, satisfaction guaranteed, special rates for block bookings and hen parties.'

'The Barmaids weekly!' Repeated Wee Mick.

Mig noticed he had an in, while half smiling at Colin.

'My advert covers half of the back page. Surely you've heard of the 'Barmaids weekly' wee man?'

Mick the mouth looked confused, Colin was right in there.

'Did you not see last weeks copy, topless pictures of Scary Spice?'

'I seen it, she could take your eye out with one of those. The topless pictures didn't go down too well with their manager though.'

'Where do you get it?' Asked the mouth

'Any News Agents' Replied Colin.

'But they do keep it under the counter' Added Mig.

"Just wait till the shop's quiet and give the guy the wink — there's all sorts of interesting stuff in it.'

'Are you going to phone her?' Asked Colin.

'No, I'm more into the direct approach, I'll go in and see her and this time next week I'll tell you how she measures up to the other twenty three.'

'Twenty three! You must be exaggerating.'

The grin on the big man's face suggested this might not be the case, he decided to crack a joke.

'Did you hear the one about the short sighted Circumcisionist?

Pauses for best effect. 'He got the sack.'

Colin and the Creature both laughed. Mick just looked confused while asking.

'What's a circum cyclist?' Another opening had just presented itself.

.'Nothing that you need to worry about wee man.'

'Well not yet anyway.' Added Colin.

'No, the problem will start when he starts putting it about, or tries to marry in to the wrong family.'

'I've heard it's part of the pre-nuptial agreement.'

Pre-nuptial agreement.' Repeated the confused one.

'That's pre-nookie to you wee man.'

The confusion was turning to concern. Mig decided to turn it up and acted as though he was talking to Colin.

'It wouldn't be for me, think about it, bits of your tackle surgically removed.

Colin grabs at his groin in mock agony. Ouch!'

Michael's concern is growing.

Colin's turn. 'It's not that... With all this date rape malarkey you keep hearing about most of the girls out there would be expecting you to sign something before they would let you anywhere near them.'

Mig grimaces and shakes his head gravely. 'Surgical removal though.'

Young Michael's concern has turned to panic; he could no longer contain himself and blurts out.

'I'm not signing anything that's going to get bits cut off my tackle....'

'Oh dear!' Said Mig.... 'Looks like he might die a virgin...'

The look of horror on wee Mick's face was priceless. Everyone was helpless with laughter drawing the attention of the supervisor.

'Right, get on with it; you're not here for a carry on.'

'You're a wee ugly prick...'

'I heard that McGuire.'

The deadpan expression is fixed firmly in place.

'You what?'

'Don't come the innocent with me. I heard you, you called me a prick.'

Wearing his very best flabbergasted look.

'I'm getting falsely accused here. What I said was wee Mick's pretty thick, on account of he never got my joke.'

The supervisor was shaking with anger but wasn't a hundred percent sure.

'This is the story of my life wrongly accused and falsely convicted.'

'Try that one on the judge McGuire.'

'Don't think that I didn't! But who is the judge going to believe the lying scumbag police in their nice uniforms or an honest guy like myself who's been wrongfully arrested thirty seven times.'

'Just get on with the work!'

'What's wrong with you this morning, somebody hide your Daily Record.'

'Less of your lip and get the walls painted or I'll be having a word with the office about you.'

'Ohhh.... but the paint's not very thick...'

The Supervisor walked away shaking his head from side to side. As the painting continued it hadn't gone unnoticed that Colin was singing to himself.

'Can the Doctor not give you something for that?'

He smiled.

'Seriously you want to catch a grip, do you want our man to have a fit?'

He mimicked the Supervisor's wee lispy voice.

'There'll be no smiling, do you hear, no smiling, you're here to paint the walls, not to smile. Anymore of this looking happy and it will be warnings all round.'

'I'm in a good mood, just found out on Thursday that the wife's expecting. So if you want to join me after the shift I'm buying.'

'Congratulations! I'm sure we could manage a few. I'm assuming you've been back there since Saturday on account that Linda gave you her phone number to give to me.'

'I was in on Thursday night, we're not barred.'

'Good we can celebrate your good news and it'll give me a chance to see hot little Linda. Any news on Moncreif?'

'His two mates were telling me he was in the General with concussion. Oh and I was to tell you that they weren't going to do anything, they were just there.'

'They weren't going to do anything my arse. If I'd been the one on the floor they would have been playing football with my head. I'll deal with them when I see them.'

Colin grinned. 'I thought that might be the case.'

'I'll need to go back to my flat first to get some money and ditch the car. The pub is about a ten minute walk from my place.'

The shift finally over they pull up outside a block of tenements.

'I'm second up on the right, come on up.'

The first thing Colin noticed upon entering the flat was a long plank notched at one end that sat diagonally up the wall.

Mig explained. 'That's for security, when I go to bed at night I wedge it between the letterbox and the opposite wall. When you live on your own you can't be too careful.'

He marvelled at the practical simplicity of the device.

'This wee place does for me.'

The short tour followed in the form of Mig opening the doors and pointing.

'My Kitchen, my Bathroom, my Bedroom and my Living room — everything I need.

The flat was tidy and organised, not what you would expect of a Bachelor flat. Above the double bed in the bedroom hung a large brass fan.

'What is that all about?'

'That's for when I'm entertaining the ladies, because when you're a rampant sex machine like myself the last thing you want is for your arse to go into meltdown half way through the action.'

Colin could visualise wee Linda under that fan in the most compromising of positions.

'Grab a seat I have something that I wanted to show you'

He handed Colin the local paper, it was open at the second page. An article had been circled.

LOCAL MAN ATTACKED
Twenty-five year old father of two Gordon McPhee was attacked outside his own home between ten-fifteen and eleven o'clock on Thursday night. Mr McPhee who works as a security guard for 'Look Sharp' security was savagely beaten about the head and body with a blunt instrument. Police are looking for witnesses to this seemingly motiveless attack and have asked that anyone who was in the area of Kintyre Avenue at that time and seen anything that might have been suspicious to come forward.

Colin had mixed feelings about this, on the one hand the testimony McPhee gave at his trial could have sent him away, on the other hand, fuck it what other hand the bastard deserved it. He read from the article.

'Beaten around the head and body with a blunt instrument.'

'Blunt instrument, I was in a good mood that night.'

He was more than slightly concerned that he had not been consulted on this.

'You didn't have to do that.'

'You're a mate and mates look out for each other.'

The ten minute walk to the pub had taken five minutes. As they entered the bar the place went quiet but they pretended not to notice. Colin ordered two pints and two whiskies.

As Colin paid for the drinks Mig lifted his pint and drained a third of it's content then placed it back on the bar.

'Looks like the head has settled on your pint.'

Linda lifted the glass and refilled it to its previous level; the big man was straight to the point.

'When is your next night off?'

There was a twinkle in her eye.

'If I make phone call I can maybe swing it for tonight, be back in two ticks.'

As she made her way to the pay phone at the end of the bar they were approached by a man in his late fifties who walked slowly with the aid of a stick.

'Is this the guy that battered Moncreif?'

'It is… This is Tam McGuire, Mig this is Willie Moffat.'

Moffat changed his stick from his right to his left hand and shook Mig's hand, he noticed Linda returning.

'A double whisky for this man.'

The drink was poured and paid for . Mig was puzzled. 'Thanks?'

'You done me a big favour son, that bastard bust my son's nose a few months back, over a game of dominoes. He got such a fright I have hardly been able to get him to leave the house since.'

Mig looked at Linda then back at Moffat.

'I have a feeling I might be seeing quite a lot of this place. So you can tell your boy from me, he won't be getting any more trouble from Moncreif.'

Linda liked the sound of this.

'After the way you beat him up I doubt if he will ever show face in here again.'

'They took him out of here on a stretcher.'

Added Moffat, enthusiastically. He continued.

'Blood pouring out of his head and stinking of piss. I would have paid a hundred pounds to have seen it happen.'

'You're welcome!'

'Anyway, thanks again.'

He headed off at a slow pace back to his table. Linda explained.

'His boy's a bit slow, totally harmless, he accidentally chapped when he could play and Moncreif started laying into him, it was a pure liberty.

'Bastard!' Added Colin.

'I wanted to bar him at the time, but the manager let him off, in case the pub windows got it again.'

The big man had other things his mind.

'So are we on for tonight?'

'Big Caroline said she would swap with me her man has a works night out tonight.'

'Good, where would you like to go; pictures the pub, dancing?'

'The pictures sounds good I've been wanting to see that new one 'Titanic', we could meet here , say about half seven.'

'I'll be here at half seven.'

They took up residence at a nearby table, Mig raised his glass.

'Here is to your good news.'

They touched glasses and drank.

'She's over the moon, talks about nothing else.'

'You can't blame her, they get like that.'

'I'm not complaining. I'm just not sure I can handle another seven months of it.'

Mig looked smug. 'The joys of married life.'

'It has its advantages, besides I'm quite looking forward to being somebody's daddy.'

This wasn't something that the big man could really relate to, time to change the subject.

'Where were you at quarter past ten on Thursday night?'

'Actually I was round here at the off sales. I had run out of fags and had missed the ice cream van. It was Linda that served me.'

'That's good, because when the security guard gets his head back together the police are going to be asking who had a motive.'

'I've been questioned by the police before, I know the score and thanks again the bastard was well due whatever you did to him. I'll do the same for you sometime.'

Colin had said this figuring that someone like Mig would always take care of their own business.

'What did you hit him with?'

As the pints flowed so to does a graphic description of every blow and cry of pain as he had let loose with a shortened pick axe handle. The initial blow to the back of the neck that had put him down, the arms the legs, the ribs, the face, the kick in the balls for good measure and the disposal of the weapon down a drain half a mile away.

Colin was enjoying hearing it almost as much as Mig was enjoying telling it, he had also liked the way the pub had gone quiet when they had walked in.

'I owe you for this; if there is anything I can do for you, just ask.'

Mig looked thoughtful for a moment.

'There was something I was going to ask you, not so much a favour more of a business proposition.'

'Fire away!'

'How would you feel about helping me sell a wee bit of blow?'

This was a well timed loaded question, after the near miss of the last time he had promised himself he would never again break the law. But he did feel beholden to Mig and figured coming straight out and saying no might not go down too well.

'Do you mean as a one off?'

'No, I mean as a steady wee business, we would be partners' fifty-fifty.'

He was looking for an out. 'Where would we get it?'

'Leave that to me.'

'What about the ones who already deal it, would they not give us trouble?'

'That one's already sorted.'

Time for a different approach.

'Why would you want me as a partner? You're obviously well capable on your own. I mean, don't get me wrong, and if it's money to get you started that's no bother.'

'It's not money; we go fifty-fifty on the set up, same with the profits.'

Colin felt uneasy. Mig was talking as though it had already been agreed. Ground was being gained.

'The reason I want a partner is that every now and then the police go out of their way to keep an eye on me. You on the other hand are almost squeaky clean. You can afford to half me on the set up, and even though I have only known you a couple of weeks, I've already sussed that your a lot smarter than most of the guys that I've ever met.'

He was flattered by this and made the mistake of smiling. Mig picked up his glass and extended it across the table in the gesture of a toast.

'We have a deal then?'

As though moved by a power he was trying to repress Colin found himself touching glasses and saying... 'Cheers!'

The big man was grinning from ear to ear.

'The way I see it, if folk want their drink and fags they can go to the pub or the off license, but for their wacky backy they'll come to us. A scheme the size of this one has a big appetite and they need a supplier. Don't think on it as breaking the law; just think on it as serving the community.'

CHAPTER 5   HIS MATES CALL HIM CHOPPER

Sunday morning, Mig was exhausted. The previous nights drinking added to wee Linda's demanding appetite had seen to this. All he wanted to do was sleep, this wasn't about to happen. He had been pacing the floor since he had taken her home at four-thirty this morning it was now ten-thirty and still the amphetamines hadn't wore off. He phoned Colin, who right at that moment was thoroughly enjoying the long lie that was denied him six days of the week. It was Marion who answered — the phone being on her side of the bed.

'Tam who?'

'It's for you.'

Looking none too pleased she handed over the receiver. He pressed the phone tightly against his far ear which wasn't easy as the wire was at full stretch.

'One o'clock. Okay, I'll be there.'

He leaned across and put the phone down.

'What was that about?'

Wearing the look of a man who had just been rumbled by the thought police.

'It's just one of the guys that I do community service with, he's going to look at a motor and he wants me there for a second opinion.'

'Oh... a motor you say... just what kind of motor and where is it?'

Colin hesitated; this was obvious proof of guilt.

'Don't you lie to me Colin Spears. I know when you're up to something, that wee smirk on your face gives you away every time.'

If at that moment his life had depended upon it he would still have been unable to control his facial expression, she caught him out with that one every time. He was at a loss for words his wife was not.

'Going to look at a motor... Do you think I'm daft and what are you thinking about, hanging around with that nut job McGuire?'

50

'The guys all right…'

'The guys all right…' Echoed Marion.

'The same guy chased Davie McNab the full length of the High Street with a broken bottle.'

'Your cousin has that effect on a lot of people.'

Realising that she might have to concede that one she chose a different angle of attack.

'So just where are you going, what are you up to and maybe more to the point just when can I expect to see you back? It was after nine when you staggered in here last night and don't you go thinking I'm going to wear that one now that I'm pregnant. Because you're not on……'

Turning over he tried to ignore her

'Whatever it is, if that guy is involved, it'll all end in trouble, oh and another thing.'

He jumped out of bed and started rapidly putting his clothes on.

'I don't need to listen to this.'

'That's right Colin, you run away.'

She grabbed the Tasmanian Devil digital alarm clock and pointed at it.

'That would be about right; the pubs will just about be opening by now.'

He hated that clock.

'Listen you… I'm a man and I don't need to answer to a woman.'

There was a sudden sarcasm in her tone.

'Oh, you're a man are you, well maybe you can be really macho and make your own tea tonight…'

Colin was losing and he knew it, he was heading noisily down the stairs, she was in full flow at full pitch.

'Mind and slam the door, we don't want to disappoint the neighbours.'

Half an hour and two cash line machines later he knocks on Mig's door.

'I wasn't expecting you so soon, come on in.'

'How was the date?'

'It was a good night we had a couple in the pub then we went to the pictures that Titanic the effects were spot on but it was really a woman's film.'

'And?'

'And what?'

'Did she come across?'

'No she didn't.' Mig was lying.

He had a sudden flashback to the back row of the cinema massaging his way up the inside of her thigh. Smooth nylon had given way to warm flesh she had moaned softly and relaxed her knee's.

'You can't always expect too much on the first date. Even if you are fifty quid lighter by the end of the night. Anyway talking about money, do you have it?'

'Pink twenty's and brown tenners do?'

'Scottish Express, that'll do nicely sir!'

Mig was grinning from ear-to-ear; his new found partner was a bit more dubious.

'Who am I going to sell it to?'

'Don't worry about that, there's no shortage of punters out there. I'll bet half the guys in your work are partial to a wee puff. Couple of things to remember though. It's not you that sells it; you might just be able to get them some. That way they can't ask you for tic and don't sell from your house otherwise you will end up with all sorts of wee dafties coming to your door at all hours.'

'Where are we getting it from?'

'It's a guy a done time with down south.'

'How did you end up doing time down south?'

'Because I was stupid'

'A friend had called in a favour'

'So there I was, driving along the fast lane, doing about eighty-five, when the traffic police flashed me. Looking back I should probably have pulled over and bluffed it.'

'But you never?'

'Not really my style. So I put the foot down. I gave them a good run for their money but even with the 2.8 under the bonnet the Capri wasn't losing the 2.7 Rover fast back'

'You got time for speeding?'

'There was more to it than that. The police searched the car and found something that shouldn't have been there. Anyway he's coming up today between one and two. He's a Biker, his mates call him Chopper.'

Colin found this slightly amusing. 'Because he rides a Chopper, right?'

'No, they gave him that name because he once set about a guy with a meat cleaver.'

He was speechless.

Mig continued.

'The guy's brand new; when we were in Durham we looked out for each other. We both got released at the same time, what a weekend that was, I met a few of his mates; nutters to a man; they were into everything; protection, drugs, guns you name they were into it. He runs with a chapter called the Scorpions. He keeps an open razor in his back pocket and a sawn-off twelve bore under the saddle of his bike. You'll like him.'

The colour drained from Colin's face as he struggled with the logic of this.

'If he's your mate maybe he would prefer to deal with you on your own.'

'Don't be daft; I'll introduce you to him. Just be polite and if he shows you his bike say something nice about it. One guy suggested that it was a bit over the top. Chopper got a bit miffed and took a crow bar to the cunt's knee caps.'

Mig found this amusing. Colin did not.

'I'll be back in a tick I'm just going to have a quick shave there's cans in the fridge, help yourself.'

As he opened the can he wondered just what the hell he had gotten himself in to. It was all happening too quick, yesterday it was pub talk but today it was already starting to happen. Mig was dodgy enough on his own but this Chopper character sounded like a real cracker and just to add a little domestic interest before anything happened at all Marion had already sussed that there was something going down.

Returning home later was not something that he was particularly looking forward to. Fuck it; he would be fortified by a few pints by then. She would have probably have went round to visit her friend Mary. That poisonous bitch 'Mary the Man'. The one who's live in boyfriend had shot through the year before without leaving a forwarding address leaving a bitter twisted bitch even more bitter and twisted. The guy obviously had his reasons for leaving but Marion had not seen the funny side of it when he had suggested that they might have been her face her attitude and the ever increasing size of her arse.

Since Stan had left Mary had lived alone with her dog Wee Willie a small Yorkshire terrier with a nasty attitude. Hr could picture them now sipping tea, with Mary giving it. 'oh no Marion surely he's not hanging around with that McGuire one, well the things I've heard about him and you in your condition too.'

Mig reappeared ready to go. Colin drained the remains of the can reflecting that there was nothing like a cold can of beer to take the edge off your worries.

'Where are we meeting him?'

'The Wee Barrel, he'll be there between one and two. There's another thing you should know about him. He looks like a greaser but he talks dead posh, don't laugh.'

'Don't worry!'

'He's alright, his real name's Tristan.'

'I can see why he would be happy to ditch that one.'

'He was educated at Oxford. His folks are loaded.'

'So how the fuck did he end up being a Hells Angel?'

'Interesting story, ask him when you see him.'

The ten minute walk to the pub had taken five minutes. A rather tired looking Linda pulled the pints avoiding eye contact with Mig for fear of revealing the guiltiest of secrets. The pub was quiet only Wee Willie Moffat and a few die hard Sunday morning regulars. The hair of the dog brigade.

'Game of pool?' Suggested Colin.

Mig fumbled for change.

'Why not say a fiver a game.'

'I used to play for the pub team.' He warned.

'I have been known to play a game or two myself.'

Having won the toss it was Colin who broke, potting one of the stripes; he then proceeded to pot the rest of the stripes narrowly missing potting the black.

Mig winked at Linda who for lack of anything else to do was watching the game. He circled the table twice, examining the angles, and then proceeded to clear the table.

'Another game?'

Colin had seen enough and declined the offer. The fiver changed hands and they sat at their usual table they were halfway through a second round when Chopper entered the pub. All eyes were drawn to the outlandish stranger, his red hair was tied back; he had full beard and moustache, wore round rose tinted glasses and the back of his jacket bore the legend Scorpions. In his hand he carried a black German helmet with a white skull and cross bones on either side.

'That's him here.' Said Mig

Getting to his feet he crossed the room. Meeting Chopper at the bar they shook hands.

'Linda, could I have a double southern comfort with ice and another two pints of lager please.

Linda started to get the order.

'How touching, you remembered my favourite tipple.'

'How could I forget that weekend we got out of Durham, we must have done a gallon of it between us — are we for a seat.'

'If it's all the same to you I would rather stand. Trade secret, after a few hours on the road the easy rider thing tends to convert to sore legs and back ache.'

Colin joined them at the bar. His first impression was one of amusement he was finding it difficult to believe that this cultured, well educated tone was actually coming from this grisly looking biker. He was introduced.

'Chopper this is my mate Colin.'

Chopper shook his hand with vice like grip.

'Pleased to make your acquaintance.'

'How long has it been?'

'It has to be at least a year and a half, and pleased as I am to see you again, I'm thinking business first. I have the express delivery package that you were expecting that's assuming of course that you have the dosh to pay me with.'

Mig wanted to take the discussion outside.

'Do you still have the same bike?'

'Of course it's in the car park come out and I will show it to you.'

Seconds later they were in the car park admiring a true work of art on wheels. The fuel tank was gleaming black with a mural of a naked woman riding a similar bike, emblazoned in fire underneath were the words *'BORN TO RUN'* the rest of the bike was covered in chrome. The forks had been extended and the rear suspension removed; three exhaust pipes fed out from the side of the engine. Colin walked round the bike — it was the same on the other side and he couldn't help but comment on this.

'Fuck sake! It has six cylinders'

The proud owner smiled. 'Why do things by half measures?'

'The 'Born to Run' is almost twenty years old. It started life as a Honda CBX 1,000 It's taken me seven years and a serious amount of dosh to create what you see before you and no, it's not for sale.'

'I'll bet it can shift.' Commented Mig.

'It gets the standing quarter mile in less than twelve seconds, top end is a shade under one hundred and forty, not competitive by today's standards but easily fast enough to lose the piggy mobiles. Anyway I never came all this way so we could stand here admiring the pretty hog.'

The hint was taken. .Money and goods changed hands. However, Chopper was still in business mode.

'Should you find yourself requiring any class A substances, I will need two days notice — same deal cash on delivery.'

'Not at the present time, I promised one of the local boys that I wouldn't interfere with his market.'

'Listen Mig, if there's a problem with this guy, just tell me and for a reasonable fee, I'll bring the Chapter up, and have a wee word.'

'I really appreciate the offer but the guy isn't anything I couldn't handle myself, it's just that now's not the time.'

'Who better to know these things than you? But if you do change your mind don't hesitate to phone me, after all what's a couple of grand a week when it could be a couple of grand a day.'

Colin stood there in silence horrified by the implications of what he had just heard. Noticing the tension Mig suggested another round and soon they were back in the pub glasses in hand.

'Colin was wondering how you came to be a Hells Angel.'

Chopper stared into the gold contents of the whisky glass, almost as though it were some kind of crystal ball.

'I was born in London, Mummy and Daddy had plenty of dosh and plenty of upper middle class values. Well I suppose you have to take the good with the bad. As for myself I was brought up so proper; insulated from the real world. I had the best of everything went to fee paying schools; Oxford, my whole life mapped out for me.

I was on the last year of my degree course — studying economics. Daddy was well connected and had already lined up a well paid job in the city for me. In short, I was doomed to live out a boring life; living and working among the stuffed shirts. Then fate stepped in.'

He drained half the glass before continuing.

'It happened one lunch time I was sitting in my favourite wine bar sipping G and T's with a couple of my classmates when in came these four ruffians, you know the type national front tee shirts bovver boots no hair no brains.'

'It started with a barrage of insults then they started throwing beer mats. My friends not being the most heroic people one could have hoped for tried to ignore them in the hopes that they would go away. One of them came over and punched my friend Nigel in the face, busting his nose. Angered by this and having no desire to be the next victim, I did the logical thing and glassed the bastard. As he stood there screaming and clutching his face, I approached his colleagues who very quickly ran away. In that moment I was hit with the sudden realisation that I was harder than they were.'

'The next thing I know I'm on remand in the Scrubs. The up side to this was that for once in my life I had time to think for myself. The experience completely changed my outlook. There in the prison I felt a very different kind of freedom. Freedom from my parents, freedom from my peer group, freedom from the heights of other peoples expectations. That was when I met Bowser and fell in with the Scorpions. Their philosophy was refreshingly similar to the way I had started to think. If you are strong enough why not just take the things you want. The chapter simply don't recognise the rules that govern other people's lives with a pack sixty-five strong they don't have to.'

CHAPTER 6   WHAT AND SPOIL THE SURPRISE

Thursday night stopping time, walking through the factory to clock out Colin was reflecting that it had been a good week. Since word had got out he could supply he had never been so popular. Popular with everyone except of course his wife who had hardly spoken two words to him since the blow out on Sunday morning. Even this had worked out to his advantage keeping up the cold air of stubborn silence meant she had not questioned why he had been late home from work every night. Obviously assuming that he had gone to the pub which in fact he had done but not before going round to Mig's to drop off money and pick up supplies.

It was working out well Mig was cutting and weighing and he was selling. The big man had been right, there was no shortage of customers, and even the few who had been given the nod were buying for friends and family. It was easy money. Passing the loading bay he met McKenzie who gave him the thumbs up.

'Same again for tomorrow'

'Sorted!'

As he stamped his card he smiled to himself. Thursday night, stopping time and laughably irrelevant, the wages were in the bank. Time for a pint everything was on the up. Even Marion was starting to give ground when he had left for work this morning she had inquired if he fancied kippers for tea. As usual the pub was quiet for that time on a Thursday Linda greeted him with a smile an empty pint glass and a friendly.

'Usual.'

'How did you know?'

They both laughed.

'How are things with you and Marion?'

'Fine, I mean we have our moments but I can't complain.'

'Since I started in here I have hardly seen her.'

'How long have you worked here?'

'Nearly two years, my original plan was to work here part time at nights and go to college to learn hairdressing.'

'Why didn't you?'

'Part time turned to full time and full time turned to over time. Sometimes I feel as though I actually live in the place.'

'Any time I'm in you always look happy at your work.'

'It's part of the job description, service with a smile.'

'Has anybody told Caroline?'

'Caroline's been here twelve years trust me she doesn't have a lot to smile about. Smiling gets harder as the night goes on, as all the ugly older men start turning in to Romeo's and the clumsy chat up lines get less and less subtle.'

Colin sympathised.

'There's more than a few of them in here.'

'Tell me about it. I'm obliged to stand here with a straight face while listening to grown men having serious discussions about UFO'S or the existence of the Loch Ness monster.'

'They're not paying you enough.'

Funnily enough that's what I've been saying to Ian for quite a while now.'

He was suddenly latched onto by Hodgey and Dodgey who judging by the state they were in had probably been at it since dinner time. They bought him a pint and were being overly friendly. They moved to a table away from the bar and their motives soon became clear.

'Going to sell us a bit for a joint.' Asked Hodgey.

His immediate thought however was, 'who the fuck told these cretins?'

'Keep your voice down for fuck sake.'

He hesitated, swayed only by the fact that they had just bought him a pint.

'Wait a couple of minutes then follow me to the gents.'

On his return from the toilets he went to the bar to buy fags.

'What are they two all about?' Inquired Linda as she gave him his change.

Time for a plausible lie.

'They're trying to persuade me to talk your boyfriend out of beating them up.'

'Boyfriend! I haven't seen Mig since you were in here on Sunday.'

'He said he would meet me in here tonight. I'm surprised he's not here yet.'

'Will that not be a bit of a shock for Dumb and Dumber over there?'

Colin grinned evilly. 'Do you think I should tell them?'

'What and spoil the surprise.'

He returned to the table.

'Have you seen Mig?' Asked Dodgey nervously.

'I saw him at the community service on Saturday. He never mentioned you two to me. So I thought it better not to bring it up, the longer it goes he might forget about it.'

Dodgey was looking uptight, Hodgey was not he was looking just a bit too relaxed. The cretin had obviously skinned up and taken a few puffs, the toilets would be stinking of it. Looking even more stupid than usual he started to talk.

'I got community service last year. Eighty hours they gave me.'

He was laughing as he spoke.

'What did you get it for?' Asked Colin.

'I got sent on one of those YOP schemes. Working in a car wash.

A tenner a week on top of your Giro. Adolf Hitler looking over your shoulder but if you don't go they will stop your Buroo money.'

'Tough at the top'

'Tell me about it! There I was working my arse off. The sun beating down on me while the smug bastards in the suits are standing around discussing interest rates and sniggering while Coonta Kintae here is polishing up their Mercs and BMW's.

This is the shite I'm putting up with for a poxy tenner on top of my Giro. The mistake they made was letting me handle the money.'

'Don't tell me, let me guess you improvised?'

'Too right I improvised. Started off I was bumping him for a pound on every tenth motor.'

It wasn't difficult to see the plot 'Then you got greedy?'

'Then it was every third Motor.'

'How did they catch you?'

'The sun was beating down the sweat was pouring off of me. Then the owner noticed that I wasn't moving very fast.' He paused for a moment.

'Having fifty pounds worth of pound coins down your wellies does tend to slow you down a bit.'

Colin almost choked on the mouthful of lager he was drinking.

'I didn't realise that I was in the company of a criminal mastermind.'

'Criminal, criminal... Ten pounds for a weeks work. That's criminal. Then when you try and get yourself a fair wage they hit you with community service and make you work for nothing; with the threat of the jail hanging over your head. Kind of makes you realise just what a good deal you had back at the Car Wash'.

'Not that I can talk...'

'But you were stealing from your Employer.'

'The bastard who owned the place was running about in a top of the range Mercedes with a private plate his wife had a BMW convertible; he's getting his workers for a tenner a week and I'm the one who gets done for being dishonest!'

Much as he disliked Hodgey he was forced to concede that he might have a point.

'Classic case of the rich using the system to exploit the common man.'

'I got my own back on the bastard. Seen the Mercedes sitting parked in the High street. I recognised it from the number plate. So I casually strolls up to it and took my Yale key to the nice shiny metallic blue paintwork.'

Hodgey swells with pride.

'I never missed a panel. I heard it was cheaper for him to front up a grand for a full re-spray than to put it through the insurance and lose his no claims.'

Colin was less than impressed.

'How's big Chas?'

Dodgey looked spooked by the question as though it had reminded him of something that he was trying to forget.

'He's still a bit shaky. Still can't remember it happening. McGuire is some piece of work. Bang; in with the head; bang the one wall; bang the other wall — threw him about like an empty track suit. We've seen big Charlie in umpteen fights he never loses, but Mig took him out like he was nothing. Then he pulls out a blade and starts coming for us. We were out of there.'

'I know the two of you nearly run me over on the way out.'

'Nothing personal Colin at that point it was every man for himself. Does he ever come in here during the week?'

Fighting hard to keep a straight face.

'He said that he might take a run in tonight.'

Dodgey slapped Hodgey on the shoulder.

'Time we were leaving!'

'When I finish my pint.'

'Make it quick will you.'

Panic was starting to set in. Hodgey was taking his time.

'In case you have forgotten. The last time we seen Mig he was going to knife the two of us.'

Just at that moment almost like a Demon summoned by the mention of it's very name Mig entered the pub. Colin got up and met him at the bar.

'A pint?'

'I'll have a pint. What are you doing sitting with that pair of Fannies?'

'They're customers.'

The big man viewed the potential victims; the look on his face said it all.

Linda placed the pint on the bar.

'Looks like they two are about to have a panic attack.' She commented.

'Unfinished Business.' Growled Mig.

Colin attempted to defuse the situation.

'Give them a break. I've been talking to them for the last half hour and I seriously doubt that they have half a brain between them.'

'I could break their heads open and we could find out for sure.'

Linda laughed. 'You just calm down. I was the one who had to mop up the blood the last time.'

'We'll see how it goes.'

As Mig approached the table they got to their feet. Dodgey the smarter of the two by a long shot had been assigned full diplomatic duties.

'Listen Big Man. We never actually did anything. We don't want any trouble.

'We're just leaving.'

'Not just yet your not.'

He placed his pint on the table.

'So you can park your arses back in your seats.'

Realising that this was not a request that was likely to be made twice they both sat down. Mig was in a playful mood.

'Here's the deal girls. I'll let the two of you walk out of here tonight but when you see Monkey you tell him from me that if he ever gets in my way again he's going to have his face removed.'

'I'll tell him that, I'll tell him that the first time I see him.'

Replied Dodgey who was pure white and visibly shaking.

'Can we go now?' There was a hint of sarcasm in Hodgey's voice.

This was not lost on Mig.

'You can go you can go to the bar and buy me a half.'

'Whisky or Vodka.'

Asked Hodgey realising his mistake.

'Southern comfort lemonade no ice and don't be long.'

Hodgey quickly made for the bar. Mig addressed Dodgey.

'What I said goes double for you and your boyfriend there.'

'Don't you worry big man I'll not be getting in your way. I might hang around with a couple of reprobates but I'm not totally stupid.'

'Just count yourselves lucky. I'm in a good mood tonight.'

Even as Dodgey breathed a sigh of relief over at the bar, events were taking an unfortunate twist. Hodgey receives his change from Linda and examines it looking confused.

'That was a tenner I gave you.'

'I'm sorry but I can assure you it was a fiver.'

'It was a ten pound note!'

Hodgey's raised voice had caught Mig's attention.

'If you want you can come back at closing time when we tally up.'

Mig got to his feet. Colin lowered his head and put his hand over his eyes.

'Listen you, you wee Slapper….'

The sentence was cut off short by the resounding crack of the bar stool as it caught him across the side of his head.

CHAPTER 7   THAT'S SERIOUS MONEY

Saturday morning yet again another shift to get through, putting even more paint on the dull, paint sucking, walls. Colin was pissed off Mig was agitated.

'Did you hear that one? The wee ugly prick reckons I'm not looking so fresh this morning. Well neither would he if he'd spent most of Thursday night Friday morning in the holding Cells.'

'What's going to come of that?'

'I told them nothing and I'm assuming no one else did either otherwise they would have had something to hold me on.'

'You don't take any prisoners.'

'Not my style!'

The established means of breaking the tedious boredom that was the heart and soul of community service had just arrived. The Michael had landed.

'How's it going Wee Man?'

Mick cringed. 'Alright.'

He replied in his best macho tone.

'I expected to see you carrying a copy of the Barmaids Weekly.'

Mick went red in the face only half an hour earlier his attempt to purchase the Barmaids Weekly had resulted in a big burly shopkeeper shouting at him to...

'Fuck off out of my shop, you wee poof and if you wink at me again I'll kick your balls.'

The wee man said nothing, the look on his face told Mig everything he had to know.

'No Barmaids Weekly, too bad, never mind.'

He put his arm round Michael's shoulder and turned him to face Colin.

'I heard from a reliable source that young Michael here got his hole last night.'

Pauses for best effect.

'It seems his fingers went right through the toilet paper.'

The Supervisor looked out from behind his paper.

'I don't know what's going on over there McGuire but it doesn't look much like painting to me. So let him go and get on with it.'

Mig put on his best homosexual tone.

'It's not what you think, we're just good friends.'

Face on fire Mick tore away rapidly.

'I'm warning you. Just get on with it and before you start. I know the paints not quite as thick as you are.'

'Clock that one Colin. It only took him three weeks to come up with an answer. They're just not paying this man enough.'

'If you're not careful you're going to find yourself back at court looking at the Nick.'

'Looking at the Nick, not me, I use a safety razor.'

'Don't push it McGuire.'

With all the enthusiasm of a trip to the Dentist the painting got underway.

'He's the one that's pushing it. I might be forced to come here and put up with this shite. But at least I'm not middle aged and still living with my mother at 72 Rosevale Avenue.'

'You catch a grip there. The pricks not worth it.'

'I'm just too tired for this shite this morning.'

Colin was more optimistic.

'On a happier note it has been quite a profitable week, it's moving fast.'

'I told you, no shortage of punters. Just be careful who you sell to though. The likes of those two from the pub the other night. They're the type who would stick you in to get off with something they had done.'

Bothered by his nose Mick the Mouth had just manoeuvred into earshot killing the conversation.

'Did you hear that on the radio this morning?'

'What was that wee man?' Inquired Mig.

'The Police raided a house down the bottom scheme and seized Heroin with a street value of seventy-eight grand.'

The big man's thoughts were suddenly elsewhere.

'Just goes to show you Wee Man. You never quite know just what's going on around you.'

'Seventy-eight grand.' Repeated the Mouth.

'That's serious money!' Commented Colin.

Mig wanted rid of the Mouth.

'It'll probably make the headlines of the Barmaids Weekly.'

Colin and Mig both laughed.

'By the way Wee Man, is that aftershave I can smell?'

'Do you like it? I got it for my Christmas.'

'You're wearing aftershave to your community service! Watch yourself

'Colin. I'm beginning to think Wee Mick fancies you.'

Not for the first time that day young Michael starts to blush. The onslaught continued.

'Don't tell me let me guess. It's that 'Obnoxious' isn't it.'

'Obsession, Obsession for men.' Declared Michael.

'See Colin he's just admitted it, he has an obsession for men.'

The wee man quickly retreated to a neutral corner and started painting away furiously. Serious conversation could now begin; it was Colin who spoke first.

'Seventy-eight grand's worth of Smack. It sounds to me like someone has just gone out of business.'

'I'm pretty sure I know who. Can't understand it though. I'll be back in a minute, call to make.'

Mig went to the toilet. It was a full ten minutes before he returned.

'I was starting to think that you had made your escape down the S bend McGuire.'

For once he ignored the Supervisor and started to paint.

'Was it who you thought it was?'

He almost laughed.

'Wait till you hear this. The guy is the main supplier of Smack in this area. He brings in thousands a week. Drives a Sierra Cosworth has all the wee junkie tarts he can handle and practically lives on take away curries.'

'Who is he and how do you know him?'

'His names Andy Gallagher and I know him because every now and then I chase up outstanding debts for him. Anyway here's the joke. This guy knows all the right folk to back hand. Fuck sake when the Drug Squad arrives to bust the house he has the tea and biscuits waiting for them.'

'Somebody stick him in then?'

'Nobody I know would be that stupid. He back hands the right folk and scares the shit out of everyone else.'

'So how did they get him then?'

'That's the amusing part. He brought in more money in a week than the rest of us are ever likely to get a sniff at and still had the audacity to have his electricity meter rigged. That's what caught him out; the Electricity Board got the police to gain access to the house. Mind you there was something well shady about that one. They turned up at half five in the morning.'

'That does sound a bit suss.'

'I'm quite sure his brief will make some sort of mileage out of it when it goes to court. Not that I can see it doing him any good in the long run. Not on those quantities. In the meantime, I would say there is a gap in the market.'

Colin could feel the hair on the back of his neck stand on end. Time to change the subject. 'How's Linda?'

'Demanding.'

'That's what I like to hear.'

He had been hoping for some sordid details but they were not forthcoming.

'I'm getting worried; I'm actually starting to like her.'

'Happens to the best of us.' Warned Colin.

'Some of us even end up hitched!'

'Get yourself to fuck!'

Replied Mig, while stepping back and slapping him playfully on the back.

'You mark my words. It could even happen to you.'

'Less carry on and get some paint on the walls.'

Shouted the Supervisor while optimistically checking out the TV guide to see what the highlight of his Saturday night was going to be.

Colin mimicked his voice. 'Less carry on and get some paint on the walls.'

Mig picked it up almost loud enough to be heard.

'Come on over here and get kicked in the balls!'

'I heard that.' The Supervisor lied

'I was just agreeing with you we should be getting more paint on the walls. It's just the paints not very thick.'

The Supervisor glared. Mig just grinned. The rest of the shift seemed to drag in even worse than usual but finally it was over and they were in the pub. Colin was forced to reflect that never had a pint tasted so good. Linda smiled and Mig's mood had improved .They sat at their usual table.

'Thank fuck that shift is over.'

So saying Colin lit up a fag.

'Things could be a whole lot worse. We have pints in hand, money in pocket and we are in the right place at the right time.'

Colin didn't like where this was going. Mig continued.

'Think about it. The main man's out of the way. There's a gap in the market that's going to need plugged in a very short time and we have a supplier who can not only get us the goods but who by happy coincidence just happens to be coming up tomorrow.'

'You can't be serious.'

'Why not, you said it yourself. Serious money.'

Colin shook his head in disbelief.

'If we don't get in there quick some other bastard will. It's too good an opportunity to miss.'

'The blow is one thing but not that stuff, no way. They mug their mothers to buy it, generally die taking it and you can get up to life if you are caught dealing it.'

The big man had not wanted to hear this so pretended that he hadn't.

'I'll get on the phone to Chopper tonight. I'm sure he can fix us up.

Only thing is we will probably need three or four grand on top of what's in the kitty.'

Sweat ran down Colin's back. He had only known Mig for four weeks and in that time he had seriously injured three people that he knew of. It was definitely time to be tactful.'

'Look I can see where you are coming from and if you need it the money is there but there is no way I am selling that stuff.'

Mig was starting to get agitated.

'Well there's a surprise. I wouldn't have taken you for a shiter.'

'It's okay for you but I have a wife at home with a kid on the way. I'm not going to be much use to them if I'm banged up for God knows how long.'

'There's one hell of a lot of money to be made and it's ours for the taking.'

'I don't give a fuck how much money there is to be made. There is no way I'm touching that stuff and that's the end of it.'

'Fuck you then. I didn't need you in the first place.'

'Look Mig, I don't want to fall out with you…'

There was a look of true madness in Mig's eyes.

'No Colin…You really don't.'

CHAPTER 8   HE COULD SEE IT ALL TOO CLEARLY

Colin woke to the delicious smell of bacon and eggs. Marion stood beside the bed plate in hand.

'This is the life.'

'Just you enjoy it while you can Mr Spears because this is the sort of service that I will be expecting in a couple of months when I start putting the weight on.'

'Maybe you won't get that heavy.'

'Are you kidding? When my sister was expecting wee Danny she was like a house side.'

Marion went back down stairs to make tea. Thoughts of resumed domestic bliss and enjoyment of breakfast were to be short lived cut off cold by the unexpected ring of the telephone. Picking it up on the first ring it was as he had feared, it was Mig.

'I made the deal with Chopper last night. He's coming up between one and two. So we will need the four grand.'

Hardly had he time to take this in when a tell tale click revealed that his other half had picked up the other Phone in the living room.

'No mate I'm Colin Spears. You must have the wrong number.'

'Wrong number?'

Inquired Marion as she re-entered the room.

'It happens sometimes.'

She sat on the end of the bed.

'Mary was telling me about your mate McGuire.'

'More words of wisdom from Dogzilla?'

Marion Scowled.

'Seems he was up for attempted murder but it got thrown out because the witnesses were too frightened to show up. Are you okay you've broken out in a sweat?'

'I'm probably coming down with the flu. That unit we're painting is bloody freezing.'

Colin feared that the Phone would ring again.

'Would you do me a favour love? I'm out of fags. Would you nip round and get me some?'

'No bother. We're running low on tea bags as well.'

The second he heard the door close behind her he hit the one four seven one.

It's me I couldn't talk earlier. The Missus had picked up the other line.'

As always Mig was straight to the point.

'What about the money?'

'Four grand's not exactly Chicken feed.'

'You said yesterday that you were good for it. Chopper's already on the Road.

'Do you want to be the one that explains to him that we don't have the money?'

'I didn't say I didn't have it.'

'Look, it's not as if you'll not get it back. A couple of months from now four grand will be loose change.'

'Give me half an hour.'

'You're some man.'

He replaced the receiver. As quickly as possible he was up and dressed.

Sliding the wardrobe away from the wall he took the Stanley Knife from on top of it and cut a square hole in the plasterboard of the wall. He reached in and removed the black bin bag that he had hidden there months earlier.

The contents of the bag were emptied onto the bed. Nine wads of a thousand and one of eight hundred and fifty. The plan was simple he would take four and put the rest back and put the wardrobe back in place. The plasterboard and wallpaper he could repair some Wednesday night when Marion was at the Bingo with Mary the Man. He had been so engrossed with the task at hand that he never heard her come in until it was too late.

'What are you doing?'

The look of anger and disappointment on Marion's face cut through him.

'How come you're back so soon?'

'I forgot my Purse.'

He could have kicked himself. The purse was in full view on top of the dressing table.

'You never answered me Colin. What's going on?'

'Okay. Big Tam wanted to borrow a few hundred off me to buy a motor.

'Don't lie to me Colin if it was only a few hundred you would have got it out of the cash machines. You do have four different cards.'

His attempt at damage limitation had well and truly crashed and burned.

'So how much is it, what's it really for and if you give it to him, what makes you think you're going to get it back?'

'Look I know what I'm doing.'

She stared at him accusingly.

'It is my money!'

'Oh it's your money and here was me thinking it was our money. Our money remember, the rainy day money to cover our backs with.'

He was at a loss for words. Marion was not.

'When I think about all the night's I couldn't sleep for worrying about you.

She shook her head from side to side.

'You very nearly got time for that money and now you going to give it away.'

'It is our money. I'm just lending some of it. I know what I'm doing.'

'You know what you're doing.'

She left the room continuing as she made her way down the stairs.

'You keep going the way you are going and you will be in the jail before the baby's born.'

He replaced the bag and the wardrobe and left the house as quickly as possible heavier by the weight of four thousand pounds. Mig's flat and two cans of beer later and still the guilt was showing no signs of dissipating. The big man by comparison was on an all time high.'

'Check these out.'

He was holding a pair of skimpy see through black panties. Obviously a trophy from the night before.

'I take it you were entertaining last night.'

'You should have seen her four in the morning and she was going frantic trying to find them.'

The Phone rang Mig picked it up.

'About fifteen minutes. We'll be there. Don't worry the money's here waiting, see you soon.'

'That was Chopper. Said he will be at the pub in about fifteen minutes. If we start walking just now we should get there at the same time.'

No sooner had they reached the pub car park when Chopper pulled up this time accompanied by another four bikes, four grizzly biker's and one very shapely female. They both watched intently as she got off the back of the bike. Removing her helmet she shook loose long blond hair. Her red leather bike jacket gaped open revealing a low cut red bra visible under a see through red top. She wore a red leather mini skirt and thigh high boots.

Chopper was straight to the point.

'I have the goods if you have the dosh.'

Mig eyed up the rest of the biker's before handing over the money. Chopper had a quick look in the bag before motioning to his companions to go into the pub.

'Why all the bodies, don't you trust me?'

'Precautionary measure, what I'm carrying today has a substantially higher value than last week's cargo. I'm carrying, and in the event of the Piggies getting nosey they're blocking, and I'm off.'

Chopper handed him a plastic bag and an envelope.

'I appreciate that you are new to this. In there you will find detailed instructions on how to cut and thin. Follow these instructions to the letter and make sure you are straight while doing so. Any fatalities and you're on your own. Any you have to get rid of do it through a third party.'

'I know the score.'

'I really hope you do. One guy, on the promise of a reduced sentence, mentioned the Chapter in court and made the mistake of thinking he would be safe in prison.'

'Fuck sake Chopper, I thought we knew each other better than that!'

'Nothing personal Mig, just my standard sales pitch. And how are you Colin? You're looking rather pale.'

Colin gave himself a shake. 'I was a bit distracted by the Lady in red.'

'Lady?' Chopper laughed.

'That's a little stray we picked up a few month's ago. She took up with Bowser. Stick him thirty quid and he will lend you her for half an hour. Just make sure you use protection and keep one hand on your wallet.'

'I think I'll pass on that one.'

'She is rather a good shag actually. Never smiles though her front teeth are broken; totally shatters the illusion. Anyway this is distracting from business. My advice to you two is to get a grip on the market as soon as you can before your predecessor nominates someone else to mind the shop. Another thing, my ear to the ground tells me there is a slight chance he may make bail while they're disputing the legality of the bust.'

Mig was just about to thank Chopper for the heads up when a distraction occurred in the shape of two of the local young team who had came staggering out of the pub.

'Look at that for a machine.'

Said the taller of the two while patting the fuel tank of the Born to Run.

'I would really appreciate it if you would keep your hands off my Bike.'

The posh well educated English accent and the polite manner caused the two youths to laugh. The hand moved from the fuel tank to the handlebars. Chopper spoke again.

'I like a man with a sense of humour. I have one myself.'

In the blink of an eye he produced a medium sized spanner and cracked the offending hand across the knuckles. There was a loud scream and sooner than they had arrived they were gone.

'Look at that. The stupid bastard has gotten blood all over my forks.'

He pulled out a clean white handkerchief and mopped up the mess. Alerted by the scream the other bikers emerged from the pub ready for a fight. Chopper raised his hand.

'It's cool. Time we were leaving.'

Within seconds they were a fading roar in the distance.

'Let's get to fuck just in case they come back team handed or worse, with the police.' Suggested Colin.

Without further ado they made their way to Mig's flat pausing only to pick up a dozen cans from a nearby off sales. In the flat there was plenty to discuss.

'About yesterday. I'm sorry I got angry.'

'What I said yesterday still stands. I don't want anything to do with that stuff. I fronted you up the money to get started. That's where it starts and that's where it ends.'

Mig had it all sussed.

'Don't you worry about your money. A couple of month's from now my only money worries will be when I start running out of places to hide it.'

'Just so we're clear. I'm not selling it for you.'

'Fair enough! I'll take care of that myself. You can stick to selling the blow.'

'I'm not happy about being involved in that either.'

The big man's mood suddenly changed and not for the better.

'But you are involved in that, aren't you and you're still doing community service for being a bad boy the last time. If someone were to stick you in you would be guaranteed time. Not just that if the Drug Squad were to unexpectedly bust your house they would probably find all that money you have stashed away.'

Colin did not appreciate being threatened,

'My money's in a Building society, in my wife's name.'

'Try again, you were able to put your hands on four thousand in cash between Saturday tea time and Sunday morning.'

Colin opened another can and said nothing.

'Look how about you keep punting the blow. Even if it's just for a couple of weeks just until I can get this other wee venture up and running.'

'Only for a couple of weeks though.'

'Give it a couple of weeks and the money will be flowing in. The last time I made any real money was when I worked the door at the Kasbah.'

'That's that night club down the coast.'

'That's the place, me and the other bouncer Eric had a good thing going with the dealer's. For a wee piece of the action we would turn a blind eye to what they were doing. Anybody else tried to sell we would confiscate their stuff give it to our dealers and pocket the profits.

Working the doors we also knew when the police were likely to turn up. It was a bad week if I wasn't six hundred better off for my Thursday Friday Saturday and Sunday.'

'Is that not where that wee guy died taking the Ecstasy.'

'That is when the rot started to set in. Not too long after that happened there was a fight in the place. Some wee wideos from Glasgow came in one Saturday night. Eric's psychiatrist had prescribed him medication to curb his violent urges, but he wasn't taking it because it meant he couldn't have a drink.'

'This Guy was working as a Bouncer.' Said Colin in disbelief.

'It was the only work he was suited to. Anyway they started it and we finished it, one of them ended up in intensive care. There were no charges pressed but the police made it clear that it was unlikely the license would be renewed if we were still working there.'

'What about the guy who died?'

'The wee guy died of dehydration, what they didn't mention in the papers was that they had the water locked off in the toilets and were charging two pounds a bottle for it at the bar.

The cans continued to flow.

'What if someone you sell to ends up dead. Does that not worry you?'

'I'll get a handle on who to sell to and how much to sell them.'

'But what if you get a bad batch? Look at those six folk who died in Edinburgh last year.'

'They would have been bumped off deliberately.'

Colin could not make sense of this.

'Why?'

'Addict's over dose all the time, nobody bats an eye.'

'You just said they would have been killed on purpose. These folk were obviously paying customers. I can't see it.'

'Paying customers who were starting to attract too much police attention. They get to a point when all the police have to do is hold them till they're rattling and then follow them. It's not hard to work out where they're going to go first. Can you see it now?'

It suddenly came back to him Chopper's comment about. 'Any you have to get rid of make sure you do it through a third party.' He could see it now. He could see it all too clearly.

CHAPTER 9   HONEY I'M HOME

The conversation had run serious and the cans had run out. The decision was unanimous, back to the pub for more drink. The ten minute walk had taken fifteen minutes. The Bar was busy for a Sunday afternoon Linda and Ian the Landlord were working quickly to satisfy demand. Mig was getting impatient.

'Reminds me of that Film!'

'What Film?'

'Death in the Dessert.'

Colin smiled.

'You never know. With all this genetic engineering maybe they could come up with the perfect Bar Tender. All they would need to do is cross a Blue Arse Fly with an Octopus.'

The pint's finally appeared Linda apologised for the delay.

'Sorry, it's a bit busier than usual.'

Colin paid for the round and they sat at their usual table.

'You're lucky she's nice.'

'I don't know she has mentioned a few times that her pal Moira's getting engaged. Oh and you haven't met my mother yet. Fuck sake we've only been going out for a couple of weeks.'

He paused to take a drink from his pint.

'A blind man could read those signs.'

'You could do a lot worse. She's good looking has a sense of humour and she works for a living.'

'Next thing you'll tell me. She wears nice underwear as well.'

'That too!'

'Settling down is for Mugs. No disrespect meant.'

'None taken.'

'Why make one miserable when you can keep them all happy?'

Even as he spoke he was eyeing up a blonde two tables away. She smiled and he winked.

'There could be worse things than settling down.'

'So you would rather be home just now?'

To this there was no reply.

'I rest my case.'

The Blonde and her frumpy friend came over.

'Do you mind if we join you?' She asked.

'Not at all.' Replied Mig.

She sat opposite him her friend opposite Colin. She introduced herself.

'I'm Pamela and she's Margaret.'

'Pleased to meet you, I'm Mig.'

They looked at each other intently. She's Margaret sighed in disgust.

'I'm Colin.'

'Are you?' Was the warm welcoming reply.

She's Margaret was overweight, no dress sense, and ugly in a masculine sort of way. Colin was forced to reflect that it wasn't often you met someone who could give Mary the Man a run for her money. Pamela on the other hand, was so over done; she probably had the words 'Free Parking' tattooed across her arse.

At least it was a good pint. Busy as she was, Linda had been watching events unfold. Colin had noticed this, and when Mig went to the toilet he explained to Pamela.

'He was going out with Linda.

'Is that right.' She replied

She looked in the direction of the bar to measure the strength of the competition. Linda looked back sizing up the potential threat. When Mig returned from the gents Pamela leaned across the table towards him, one eye on Linda, to make sure she was watching.

'What's your pals name again?'

She asked this quietly causing him to push his face closer in an attempt to hear her.

'Your pals name, whisper it to me.'

Mig was puzzled but whispered it to her anyway. Pamela looked across at Linda and put her hand over her mouth laughing as though she had just heard something really funny. His attention drawn by this Mig also looked at Linda who immediately turned away looking for customers to serve.

Pamela strolled up to the Bar. The Landlord was rounding up empty glasses only Linda was serving, and she made her wait as long as she could. Pamela smiled at her holding up a tall glass with half an inch of Bacardi and Coke in the bottom of it.

'This Glass has a lip print on it. I want another drink.'

Linda took the Glass and examined it.

'It's hardly surprising that there's a lip print on it. You are wearing lipstick.'

Linda smiled coldly. Pamela examined the nail varnish on her right hand as though bored with it all.

'Just get me another drink.'

'The drink that was in it is all but finished. I'll have to wait till Ian comes back from rounding up the empties to see if you've to get one.

Pamela lit up a Cigarette.

'I remember you from School. Linda Blair isn't it?'

'That's me.'

'A Barmaid, glad to see you did so well for yourself.'

This comment was accompanied by a waft of smoke.

'I remember you from School too, Pamela Smith.'

'That's me, sweet Pamela.'

'Or as you were known to the fourth year boys' the Sweaty Palm.'

The crowd Around the Bar were starting to take an interest.

'They didn't call you 'Loose Linda' for nothing.'

The voices were starting to rise fuelling more interest from the Customers.

'You're the one who had to leave half way through fourth year because you got pregnant and your uniform wouldn't fit.'

The guys around the bar were starting to get in to the spirit of things and the last comment was followed by a chorus of. 'Oooohs!'

This seriously annoyed Pamela who decided to use the unwanted audience to best advantage.

'Mig told me you're no good at blow jobs.'

'Yes I am.'

Linda could have bitten her tongue off but it was too late already. Her face was going bright red to the sounds of laughter around the bar. The gloves were off. Linda composed herself and turned to the guys at the Bar.

'I heard she burnt herself red raw while attempting to dye her pubes to match her head.'

Pamela glared wondering how the wee bitch had found out about this.

Alerted by the slanging match Mig appeared at the bar.

'What's wrong?' He asked.

Pamela was in there first.

'It's this one here; my glass has a lip print on it and she won't replace my drink!'

'I'll buy you one. What are you drinking?'

'A Bacardi and Coke thanks.'

The points were being scored.

'Make it a double and I'll have another pint.'

A smug look was starting to spread across the Sweaty Palms face. Linda picked up a tall glass and gave Mig a disapproving look. For once his dead pan expression was starting to slip.

'I'm just trying to keep the peace.' He said, half laughing.

'If you sit back down with that Strumpet don't bother phoning me again!'

'Listen you don't own me. I'll talk to whoever I like.'

Fearing things might escalate Ian the Landlord got in with.

'Linda, just serve them their drink.'

Linda placed the drinks on the bar.

'I want ice.' Demanded Pamela.

Face like thunder Linda reached for the Ice bucket.

'She's not looking too happy.' Commented Pamela mirthfully.

'She's in a bad mood because her arse is cold.' Said Mig.

'She'll be all right when she puts these back on.'

Mig threw Linda's panties on to the bar to the serious amusement of all except Linda who was mortified. The Sweaty Palm had wanted ice, and she got it — right in the face. Linda ran out through the back door of the pub, the humiliation was too much to bear.

Colin decided it was home time. He had been drinking pretty much non-stop since domestic bliss had been shattered that morning. He was walking fairly straight but in reality he was pretty far gone. The drink had brought out the philosopher in him. He started to reflect over the previous couple of weeks. The community service the violence, drug deals, the Hells Angels and 'She's Margaret' head butting Ian the Landlord as he had came round the bar to retrieve the ice bucket.

It was all solid proof that there was no need to run off and join the circus. Since he'd met Mig the circus had come and joined him. Going home was something he would handle when he got there. Crossing the car park in front of the shopping mall he found himself in among the last gasp of the Sunday car boot sale. That's when he saw it the five piece knife set in the hardwood block. It was perfect; the block matched the colour of the kitchen units. Marion had always wanted a good knife set. Time for some hard bargaining.

'How much for the knife set mate?'

'A Fiver.'

'Done!'

Well pleased with his newly acquired peace offering he slowly made for home.

Meanwhile back at the pub it was taking three police officer's all of their time to overpower and restrain the fifteen stone whirlwind of malevolence she's Margaret.

One of them had taken a well placed knee to the groin and was showing a bit less enthusiasm than his colleagues.

Mig was helpless with laughter as they struggled to get the cuffs on the kicking and biting Margaret. Some day's it all just happens, hardly had the police dragged the screaming and shouting Margaret from the premises when in to the bar walked Chas Moncreif; for once without the usually present Hodgey and Dodgey. Mig got straight up and met him at the bar.

The whole place went silent. Moncreif's face still bore some of the bruising from their last encounter. He spoke first.

'I'm here to talk.'

'I'm listening.'

'Not at the Bar, let's sit down.'

Mig was not about to turn his back on him.

'After you!'

They sat opposite each other; the big man had one eye on the empty pint glass in easy reach of his right hand.

'I'm not looking for any trouble.' Mig said nothing.

Moncreif continued.

'Wing Nut's Criminal injuries came through and he wants to pay Gallagher what he owes him. The problem is he can't find him to give him the money and he's shiting himself in case you come looking for him again.'

He was tempted to say it's cool Gallagher's in the nick, everything all right, but what price benevolence, there was nine hundred pounds to be had.

'The Man's currently indisposed and I'm handling his affairs give it to me and I'll see he gets it.'

'Wing Nut is outside just now I will go and get him.'

Moncreif got to his feet and left.

Mig was on a roll. Gallagher was out of the way, Chopper had just brought him enough smack to corner the market and who better to punt it than Wing Nut. He knew who Gallagher's customers were, and given that he had been marked up already, he would do as he was told. Add to that a quick nine hundred pounds bonus and Pamela had promised to show him her body piercings as soon as she got back from the police station.

'Honey I'm home!'

It's a curious thing how drunk men without a leg to stand on grab bravado with both hands.

'I got you a present.'

Cold stare.

'It's something that you've wanted for a while.'

Thaw factor, try striking a match at the South Pole.

Colin produced the perfect Knife Set.

'I got this for you at the car boot sale.'

She was trying her hardest to dislike the knife set.

'Look it matches the Kitchen.'

She was tempted to comment but restrained herself. He was too pissed to be into the argument.

Humour the drunk mans best ally. Colin grabbed the biggest knife from the set. The actual weapon of choice of any psycho killer worth his salt.

He started walking round the kitchen stabbing downwards at the air while mimicking Marion's voice and re-creating sound effects from the famous Hitchcock movie.

'You're a drunken wrong un Colin Spears. But you'll pay for it now. YEEP! YEEP! YEEP! Come home to me with a broken pay will you. YEEP! YEEP! YEEP!'

Marion was fighting a losing Battle trying to keep her face straight.

'Ah ha so you are talking to me then.'

'Don't start me Colin, just don't start me.'

'Maybe I should have quit when I was ahead, when you weren't talking to me.'

'I'll talk to you when you're sober.'

'Ooooooooooh!!! Drunken wrong un YEEP! YEEP! YEEP!'

CHAPTER 10 YOU'LL FIND IT IN THE CAR PARK

It's funny how a week can drag in or fly by, depending on how your luck is going. In Colin's case it had been the cold silence, face mask on at bed time and cheese in his pieces every day. Normally it would have been gammon or turkey roast, but not this week. Mig by comparison was having a great week. Wing Nut had given him the nine hundred pounds that he owed to Gallagher, Moncreif gave a grovelling apology. Wing Nut was selling rapidly and had even passed on a couple of good tips for the Bookies he was turning out to be an asset.

Thursday night, the Wee Barrel, usual table; pints in hand and Mig was in full flow about Pamela her body piercings and the things she was up for. Things that given his current situation Colin could have did without hearing about. He figured that he would be unlikely to get lucky this side of the baby being born. His usual benevolent attitude of 'good luck to anyone else who was getting it' had disappeared along with the gammon and turkey roast.

'Cheer up for fuck sake you'll have me weeping into my drink in a minute.'

He stared at his pint and frowned.

'You shouldn't be sitting there with the face on. You should be using your time constructively.'

'Doing what exactly?'

'I don't know. Maybe we could be sitting here devising increasingly sadistic new ways to torture Mick the Mouth. You go first.'

Colin thought for a moment.

'You mean like tell him that it's just came out that The Spice Girls are all Lesbians.'

Mig smiled.

'And it must be true because you read it in the Barmaids weekly.'

'Barmaids Weekly that was a good one.'

The drink was starting to kick in and Colin was feeling a bit better.

Mig's turn.

'How about this we wait till the Supervisor is looking the other way. We grab him strip him off douse his pubes with some of the thinners we use to clean the brushes, strike a match and away we go.'

He points in the air for best effect.

'Then Wee Mick never the sharpest tool in the box is faced with a dilemma. Faced with a dilemma and not too much time to think about it. What does he do? Does he just kind of pat away, being careful not to burn his fingers while his nuts are toasting, or does he slap away hard and risk inflicting serious damage'

The image of young Michael furiously slapping at his groin did cause Colin some amusement.

'Or maybe he goes for a third option and in an attempt to stifle the blaze he grabs on tight with both hands while hobbling about screaming.'

Colin laughed. 'You're one evil bastard.'

Mock hurt look.

'In my defence it's community service, you have to do something to relieve the boredom. Besides, maybe after hearing that bad news about the Spice Girls it's what he would have wanted.'

They were approached by a young guy who had just entered the pub. He was tall and thin protruding ears stuck out under a back to front baseball cap. At some point his nose had been broken; his face had numerous small scars and on the left side there was a two inch straight line so recent that the stitch marks were still visible. He looked frightened. Colin recognised him as one of the local young team but did not know him by name or to speak to. He addressed Mig.

'Listen Big Man we've got trouble!'

Mig put his foot on the chair opposite him and pushed it out from under the table.

'Sit down and enlighten me.'

'The boys are telling me there's a couple of real hard cases going around in a big black Ford asking who's doing what on this patch and threatening to break legs when they find out.'

The big man took a drink from his pint.

'Okay! So who are we talking about?'

'I don't know for sure. Somebody said they think it's Matt Gallagher Andy's older brother. But why would he have a problem with us. I mean Andy left you in charge didn't he.'

Even as he was saying this the penny was starting to drop. Mig got in first.

'Matt's fuck all to worry about. Who's with him?'

'Two guys, they're not from around here.'

'You stick to what you are doing and don't worry about it.'

'It's Okay for you to say don't worry about it, but the doctor who examined me for the rehab said I was lucky to have survived the kicking I got in the nick last year.'

'My heart bleeds for you.'

He turned to Colin.

'Our man here had an expensive habit and how did he pay for it? He was an equal opportunity blagger, stole from family, friends, neighbours, the old folk. Totally shites on his own doorstep, then he gets caught and finds himself banged up with a few disgruntled friends and relatives.'

Mig drained his glass his mood had taken a sudden turn for the worse.

'Listen cunt, I don't want to hear it, and you had better not try 'oh they beat me up and took the stuff off me' with me. You know what happened the last time. So get to fuck out of here, and remember we're not interested in dodgy credit cards knocked off tellies, videos or toasters, just cash and no tic. If there's any trouble refer them to me.'

The boy left the pub. Colin looked at the big man; he could almost feel the madness in the air, like your hair standing on end if you walk under a pylon. Colin was just about to get the round in when Pamela walked in.

Mig got up and met her at the bar she was looking hot; stiletto heels, mini skirt split to the hip, see through blouse, short brown leather jacket. Well practiced in the not so noble art of wind up she grabbed him and kissed him passionately. Linda ran a damp cloth over the bar.

Pamela had the irritating habit of speaking to people without actually looking at them.

'A Bacardi and Coke.'

Linda ignored her. Pamela lit up a cigarette.

'Just when you have a minute.'

She turned and faced her.

'Oh! Were you talking to me?'

'No love I'm talking to the optic measures at your back. Now if you don't mind I would like a Bacardi and Coke. That's with ice.'

This was accompanied by a stream of cigarette smoke to emphasise her impatience.

'Sorry! But I'm not serving you.'

'Fine, get me the Landlord.' She said to the polished nails on her right hand.

'He's not here so I'm in charge. But if you want to come back in two or three hours.'

The Sweaty Palm scowled like a spoiled child.

'No, it's all right. Unlike some, I have other places I could be tonight other than this dive.'

Linda looked her up and down.

'You'll be going to your work then?'

The angry Pamela could not think of an appropriate reply to this so she turned to Mig and kissed him again.'

'I'll get you in Valentino's about half nine.'

Pamela turned and made for the Door.

'Who has your kids tonight?' Shouted Linda.

She ignored the question and put on a burst of speed. Mig always did have a problem with modesty and watching two women bitching over him had him grinning from ear to ear. This had not gone unnoticed by Linda.

'As for you, you big headed bastard, I thought we had something, but you. You couldn't see past the split in that wee tarts skirt.

Mig figured it wasn't his fault if Pamela had pierced nipples and a black belt in Karma Sutra.

'Could I have two lagers please?'

'Would you like to drink them or wear them?'

There was fire in her eyes. Taking the threat seriously he fought off an overpowering urge to say. 'You're beautiful when you're angry'. He returned with the pints.

'What are you looking at me like that for?'

It's not my fault if I'm lusted after by anything in a skirt. It's even been said that I'm the only known cure for Lesbianism.'

Colin lit up a fag and changed the subject.

'The guy that came in, who is he?'

'That's Wing Nut, he's selling for me.'

'I had gathered that. Why do they call him Wing Nut?'

'When was the last time you seen a pair of ears that stuck out like .'

'That's some rip someone has given him.'

Mig took a drink from his pint and placed it back on the table.

'He must have tried to get wide with the wrong person.'

'What's his real name?'

Unhappily Colin was starting to put two and two together.

'I've never asked him. He used to sell for Gallagher.'

Colin looked at his watch. 'I'll have to go.'

There was a mirthful look on the big man's face.

'What's so funny?'

'Nothing!'

'Come on what's so funny?'

The mirthful one was well aware of the matrimonial disharmony in the Spear's household.

'You wouldn't catch me running home to a scowling face.'

This comment did not go down well.

'I'm only noising you up.'

He slid a bulging envelope across the table.

'There's five hundred in there that leaves three and a half.'

Colin smiled.

'And angry woman or not; you're not going to tell me that you can't stay for another couple.'

Meanwhile less than a mile away the hapless Wing Nut totally undeterred by the big man's warning and eight weeks in rehab had been sampling the goods and was walking down the street happily oblivious to the whole world when up pulls the factory black Mk 3 Ford Granada Scorpio.

Forty five minutes later Mig's mobile rings. 'Sounds like Pamela's getting impatient.'

He answers it. 'Hello!'

> 'McGuire, just a wee call to let you know Andy has a hearing tomorrow. He's expecting to be out and about by this time tomorrow. In the meantime he's sent you a message. You'll find it in the Car Park.'

Colin followed Mig outside. Hardly recognisable for the blood; Wing Nut lay unconscious on the ground. Taken by ambulance to the accident and emergency it was one of the few times in his life that he got to be the first in the queue.

Medical examination revealed; a shattered right knee, breaks to his arms, various missing and broken teeth and a fractured skull. Suspected cause of injuries repeated impact with a blunt instrument. Educated guess, a Baseball bat.

CHAPTER 11 THE LEGION OF THE DAMMED

Three-forty-five in the morning and despite Pamela's heavy demands and the comforting smell of her earlier presence, sleep just wasn't happening. She had slid home to her so far unmentioned Children. Mig was alone with his thoughts; the phone call in the pub and Wing Nut lying in the car park smashed up. A wee message from Andy. Gallagher always did have a sense of humour; Mig recalled one time he had went round to visit him. Some young guy had come round; he already owed fifty quid and made the mistake of asking for tick. Gallagher had burst out laughing before setting the two Staffies, Ronnie and Reggie on him. As sure as trouble was coming, sleep was not.

The flat upstairs had been empty for two months, the young couple who previously lived there had moved to a bigger flat, but Mig still had the spare key they had entrusted to him to allow him to feed their cat when they were away for the weekend. Entering the Flat he rolled back the Bathroom carpet, prized up the loose floorboard and there it was his insurance policy. He removed the three shot pump action Luigi Franchi the gun had originally been stolen from a country house and traded to the Scorpions for drugs as a favour. Chopper had asked Mig to store it on the understanding that he could have the use of it until its return. The feel of the gun in his hands and its potential for destruction reassured him. Even without firing a shot the sight of the Shotgun alone would be enough to make someone shite themselves.

Seven-fifteen a.m. and all too soon the Tasmanian Devil alarm clock sounded the start of the day in the Spears household.

'Come on Colin. It's time to get up for your work!'

His mind was unwilling and his body even more so.

'Not this morning.'

'What do you mean not this morning? You're not going to hold on to a job like that.'

'Not this morning.'

He pulled the covers over his head.

'Straight to the pub from work yesterday; boozing all night with that McGuire one and now you can't make your work this morning'

This was her, the Marion that he knew and loved wielding the truth like a big stick. There was silence from under the covers.'

'They might just pay you off!'

'Murphy Packaging can do without me for one day!'

Her silence spoke volumes. The voice below spoke again.

'Between that hole and the community service I'm out six days a week.

'Even I deserve a day off now and again.'

'You had better at least phone them.'

'You phone them for me.'

'Me, phone them, and what exactly am I going to say to them. Oh by the way my man can't make it in this morning. Why is that you're asking? Oh he has a good legitimate excuse. He's lying in his bed half pissed from the night before.'

Colin was starting to entertain the notion that the bleak freezing cold shop floor of Murphy's with the screaming machines and the obnoxious gaffer might actually be the better bet.

'Going to just phone them, tell them I have a sore head or something?'

She said nothing. He took this as a good sign.

'I'll take you down the town later. You said you wanted to look at prams and things. We could maybe have a pub lunch.'

He quickly realised that his last comment had been a tactical mistake.

'Pub lunch! You're starting to spend more time in the pub than you spend in the House. Well it's not on; a few months from now there's going to be baby to consider and I have no intention of being stuck in here changing nappies while you're out there getting legless with that nutter you're hanging around with.'

'Drunken wrong un.' He muttered to himself from under the covers.

'What was that?'

'Going to just phone them?'

'I'll phone them, but it's the last time and you had better think about getting up. You're taking me down the town, remember.'

She always did drive a hard bargain.

'I could be doing with a new pair of shoes.'

The hangover suddenly intensified. 'Please God not shoes anything but shoes'. He had been subjected to the dreaded shoe shopping torture before. The unending search for just the right ones, in the right style, in the right size, at the right price, a quest that would make a marathon pale by comparison.

One last hope. 'I could give you money and you could go yourself.'

'And I could come back to an empty house and you in the pub. You're not getting off the hook that easily.'

One last hope lying dashed on the rocks of reality.

He peered out from under the covers. 'It's only half seven.'

'That'll give you plenty of time to pull your self together then and have a shave.'

By ten-thirty Colin had already seen more shoe shops and more shoes than his fragile state could easily cope with. He entertained the notion that nothing could be worse than this. Wrong again as they exited the umpteenth shop there she was Mary the Man large as life and looking uglier and more sceptical than the last time he had been unfortunate enough to have seen her — if that was possible. He braced himself, Marion and the poisonous one had not seen each other for two days which would probably equate to around three hours worth of gossip she greeted them.

'Marion how are you?'

Formalities over it was straight to the attack.

Surprised look.' Colin are you not working today?'

She turned to Marion putting her hand to her mouth with an accompanying look of mock horror.

'Oh, I haven't put my foot in it. He's not been paid off has he?'

'No he arranged today off last week.' Marion lied.

'It's just I heard that Murphy's were bumping thirty of them at the end of the month.'

Mary had noticed that Colin was looking the worse for wear.

'Course it'll be the bad time keepers and the one's who won't work overtime that'll be the first to go.'

Colin could see her angle and no she wasn't getting a reaction. Mary liked a challenge and continued chipping away.

'It's not that, jobs are that hard to find these days. That was wee Sandra's man paid off from the whisky bond and they're just like you, there's a wee one on the way.'

She leaned forwards towards Marion and lowered her voice.

'They told me he got paid off, but I got it from a reliable source that he got caught taking stuff out the back door. Oh but they're finding it tight now, now there's no money about.'

He could feel the air of poisonous satisfaction. No money about, inside his pocket he had his hand wrapped around a five-hundred pound wad of notes and at that moment he could have happily rammed it in to her mouth just to shut her up. He couldn't resist it.

'Heard anything from Stan recently?'

He had asked this knowing full well that she hadn't.

Mary looked away as though wounded by the question and Marion elbowed him in the ribs. He tried hard not to smile.

'I haven't heard from him and I don't care. With any luck the bastards caught something and died.'

'What did you do with yourself last night?'

Asked Marion, strategically changing the subject.

'Last night, that was a good one. The Pamela one from two closes down comes to my door. She's been phoned by her mother who she's not seen in years on account of some sort of family falling out. Could I watch her three kids, just for a wee while? She would be ever so grateful and there would be a tenner in it. She's standing there in an old pair of jeans and a tee shirt that's seen better days, her hair's in a mess, so I took pity on her and said I would do it.

'Ten minutes later she's back looking like she's about to star in some pop video and I find myself minding the two year old mad eyed screamer with the minging arse and no change of nappy and the two boys, five and six, who when they're not trying to beat each other senseless are trying to pull my house apart.. I comes out of the kitchen and here's the older one, he's attached himself to the radiator and is swinging himself backwards and forwards trying to pull it off of the wall.'

Colin was trying hard not to laugh.

'Anyway half three in the morning and the legion of the dammed have finally ran out of steam and guess what... Five minutes later in strolls madam, half-pissed and smiling all over her face, like she's just had a two hour session with a deluxe multi-speed. 'Oh. Look at my Wee Angels all crashed out on your Couch.' She says. This is at half three in the morning, so I'm too tired to argue. All I want is my tenner and to get to bed. But her, she wants to talk. She's well full of herself, tells me the older boy looks just like his father who, just incidentally, got wrongly lifted for supposed possession with intent to supply, which was a bit harsh because really he was just holding the stuff for someone else. Anyway she hadn't really seen him for a couple of years and she's got this new guy Tam McGuire who she really likes but out of the blue the Andy one has phoned her from the nick. Then it gets all secretive she can't say too much but he's expecting to be out by the weekend and there's going to be trouble.'

Mary looked at Colin.

'You hang around with him, don't you?'

Sudden Flash back to Wing Nut lying in the car park.

'I've had a pint with him a couple of times!'

Mary gave a sceptical look before turning back to Marion.

'Oh, and keep this one to yourself. Lizzie Anderson from up the stairs comes home early from work. Stomach cramps, know what I mean, only to catch her man in her bed with her best pal Angela.'

Mary was on top form. 'I'm telling you, it's scandalous.'

Ten minutes to midnight, Matt Gallagher and two accomplices set about Mig's door with a sledge hammer. Upon entry they are surprised to find that despite the lights being on and music playing the flat is empty. As they turned to leave there was a second surprise in the shape of Mig who had been sitting in the darkness in the flat above waiting for them to come. He was now standing on the landing Luigi Franchi shotgun poised and ready.

'Are you looking for me?'

Matt Gallagher actually pissed himself.

'Matt, get down there and tell Andy to get up here, I want to speak to him.'

Mig had seen Andy in the driving seat of the Cossy when it had pulled up outside.

Matt stood rooted to the spot...

'What the fuck are you waiting for get him up here and if you don't come back these two are getting it.'

Matt bolted down the stairs Mig's finger took up the tension on the trigger. There was the sound of the car door slamming. As Mig got to the street smoke was coming from the back tyres of the Cosworth the first shot blew away half of the whale tail spoiler. There was no point in a second shot the car was long gone as were the other two from up the stairs. Mig moved the wheelie bin and lifted the slabs and placed the shotgun in the place previously prepared put the bin back then it was across the backdoor s to Pamela's before the police appeared. He had been with Pamela all night hadn't he?

CHAPTER 12   IT WAS GOING TO BE A LONG DAY

The sound of the Sirens caused Mig to look back across the darkened expanse of the backdoors. In the distance his own close stood out, a black silhouette against the blue flashing background. The police had been quick off the mark it had been barely ten minutes since the shot had been fired. Quick off the mark yes — quick enough, no.

Entering Pamela's close from the back he was experiencing an adrenalin rush like never before. He was so mentally and physically charged he felt unstoppable. Mig checked the nameplates trying to find the right door the top landing light was out he lit a match the door in front instead of a nameplate had a piece of card attached by a drawing pin written on it in felt tip P.SMITH. He chapped the letter box at eye level a pin hole of light appeared then disappeared.

'Who is it?'

The tone was seductive, suggesting that she already knew.

'It's me!'

'Just a minute!'

The Mortise and Yale unlocked and the door opened. Pamela stood there in a red satin pyjama top that barely covered her modesty other than that, all she wore was a smile.

'I didn't expect to see you here.'

His pulse pounded even quicker. There would be time to sort out alibis and matching stories later.

'Well I'm here now.'

As they embraced he slid his left arm around her back and his right arm around the backs of her legs he lifted her off the floor. Stepping forwards he turned around using her back to close the door before pinning her against it. She opened her legs and dug her heels in to the backs of his knees.

Saturday morning again, the start of the shift and Colin was pissed off. Murphy's shite -hole that it was, at least you got paid for being there but here at the community service you worked the day for nothing other than the privilege of staying out of the jail. To add to the mood the rain had been bouncing off of the pavement all morning and there was no sign of Mig. In light of recent events Colin feared the worst.

'Where's the Big Man this morning?' Mick asked.

The Mouth was looking chipper than usual. That one could be easily sorted.

'Phoned me earlier, said he might be a bit late, probably turn up any minute.'

Young Michael s face fell. Colin noticed that the Creature wasn't looking too hot. He recognised the look, slightly spooked, half way between the drink wearing off and the paranoia kicking in. It was going to be a long day the shift began.

'Doesn't look like Mig's going to show.'

This was repeated by wee Mick every five minutes on the five minutes, punctuated by; 'what time is it now, it's dragging in?'

'It's dragging in' As though he really needed reminding of this. He looked around him maybe this really was the Twilight Zone the place where time really did stand still — an alternative reality where windows didn't exist and where, by some freak of nature, the walls could take four coats of brilliant white paint and still not look right. Trapped here in this darkest of dimensions known as community service with the other two wretched creatures the one that never speaks unless it's muttering to it's self and the other one that never seems to shut up, with the amazing ability of being able to talk shite all day long. And not forgetting the tragic old sentinel; charged with guarding the doorway lest the prisoners escape — cursed with the affliction of having it's head trapped in the Daily record for seven hours of the day.

'Doesn't look like McGuire is going to show.'

This time it was the Supervisor, his voice oozed satisfaction.

'Far as I know he was on his last legs for time keeping. Oh dear how I'm going to miss him.'

No one looked round but the painting suddenly moved up a gear.

'Course you're all on borrowed time just one unexplained absence or a wee word in the right ear from me. Just one slip up and it's off to the Big House.'

Colin new a wind up when he heard one, Michael on the other hand was barely seventeen and not so worldly wise — this had not gone unnoticed by the Supervisor.'

'Just you imagine it Young Michael just one slip up and it's a case of do not pass go. Do not collect two hundred pounds.'

Wee Mick was bright red and starting to sweat. The Supervisor was enjoying himself.

'But wait that's not the best part. My mate he's a Prison Officer, he told me that there was a big shake up recently. The Powers that be had got fed up with the amount of drugs that were getting smuggled in so they decided to implement a new policy. So now before you even make it to the showers it's on with the good old rubber gloves, knickers down, bend over and hands up.'

Sweat was running down the side of Michaels face.

'There's nothing quite like the good old cavity search. Hee hee hee!..'

The Supervisor was really enjoying himself.

'Oh and don't go thinking that these guys are gentle about this. These guys are Sadists, it's part of the job description. If you don't let out a good loud scream they don't feel they've done their job right. Professionalism know what I mean.'

Michael was almost in tears.

'Can you hear it now — the snap as the glove goes on?'

'Leave the boy alone.'

Snarled Brian Something, startling everyone not least the Supervisor.

'Fuck me it can speak!'

This was said to disguise the fact that he had nearly shit himself. He quickly retreated back to the safety of his chair and newspaper. The supervisor looked composed but Colin new what he was thinking. 'That cunt's not predictable hide behind your paper, shout out paint now and again as though you actually gave a fuck, earn your wages and go home'. Home to whatever the fuck that was?

The painting continued in silence this had an unfortunate side effect. Un-distracted by Michael's continual talking, Colin found himself at the mercy of his own thoughts and worries. He tried to make sense of how it had come to this. Okay so he had seen an opportunity to rip off Matrix Electronics for a good few grand this was a company with a ten million a year turn over. They in turn, unable to catch him, had fitted him up, sore at the time but two's up to them when he never got the Jail. This had all kind of balanced out when Mig had taken care of the security guard McPhee.

He had got community service, and could no longer say that he had no criminal record, but on the up side there was close on thirty-five grand tucked away in various places. It hadn't exactly been the 'Great Train Robbery' but it had, within reason, set him and Marion up for life.

What was really troubling him was just how complicated things had become over the last few weeks and where was Mig? Did he get it the same as Wing Nut and if that was the case was he next? He tried to reassure himself that he'd been no more than a silent partner but it wasn't working.

'Break time, you can have ten minutes for a smoke.'

The Supervisor announced, with his usual tone of charming generosity.

Michael cadged Colin for a cigarette while Rigor Mortis turned away in case it was noticed that he was shaking so bad he was having difficulty lighting his roll up.

Young Michael of a Saturday night was a big man to his little friends. He was the one who could get served in the off sales. On a Saturday night he was a big man standing in the bus shelter with the more evolved fifteen year olds getting full of it and boasting about how hard he was and how he was doing community service with this one and that one and give it five years and I'll be running this town. However this was not Saturday night in the bus shelter this was Saturday morning at the community service this was the real world and he was an ever decreasing wee boy in among the grown ups and panic had started to set in.

'He's kidding right I mean about the cavity searches?'

Silence, long drawn out, frightening silence…

'I mean he's kidding right?'

Colin was not qualified to comment on this. It was Rigor Mortis who spoke wafting the smell of raw vodka in their direction.

'He's not kidding wee man and lots of worse things happen in the nick.'

The smell of the Vodka hung heavy in the air Colin and Mick looked at each other suddenly drawn together by a mutual problem.

'Much worse things.'

He was starting to slur his words.

'Not wanting to alarm you but much worse things. See that.'

He pointed to a half inch scar just below his left eye.

'What do you think that was done with?'

Looking round, the Supervisor was as ever hid behind his paper. Brian openly produced the quarter bottle and drained the remaining third in one go.

'Well, look at it. What do you reckon, an open razor, a Stanley Knife?'

No answer was forthcoming.

'No nothing quite so sophisticated, that one was done with a broken toothbrush.'

Totally out of character Brian something AKA 'Rigor Mortis' AKA 'The Creature' was trying to communicate. The only problem was he had consumed a quarter bottle of vodka in the last ten minutes that was on top of eight super lagers six last night and two for breakfast. He grabbed the Mick the Mouth by the collar and pulled him in.

'You listen to me wee man, don't end up in the jail, bad things happen there.'

Still holding he moved back a couple of inches and made serious eye contact.

'You take it from one who knows.'

Overcome by a sudden urge to be alone Michael made for the toilet. Brian looked long and hard at Colin.

'I have some advice for you too. Do yourself a favour and steer well clear of the Big Man.'

He paused for a moment.

'See either he doesn't remember me or he's making out that he doesn't know me but I know him. I've known him since he was a boy.'

'He seems Okay to me.' Said Colin without conviction.

'He might seem all right but I know things about him that you don't.'

As the Vodka was starting to kick in the voice was getting louder.

'Keep it down, if that cunt notices you've been drinking your fucked!'

Before his very eyes he was witnessing the total character reversal.

'Who that Bastard. I'll take my chances. Getting back to McGuire.'

He paused for a moment struggling hard to remember what it was that he had started to say. Leaning forward slightly he started to poke at his right temple with his right index finger.

'Mad! I'm telling you mad. It runs in the Family.'

Colin's face gave away nothing.

'Never mentions his parents, does he?'

There was no answer to this.

'No and I'll tell you why! Going back to when he was about twelve years old his old man was much like he is now. Hard Bastard — when he wasn't actually in the jail he was prone to heavy drinking and slapping the boy's mother around. One Saturday afternoon he comes home after losing heavy at the bookies. Something snaps, he gets it with a kitchen knife. Nobody is too sure what really happened but the Mother she's taken to the Loony Bin, the boy to a children's home.'

Colin felt a cold shiver run through him.

'What about the Father?'

'Didn't make it to the hospital, rumour was he had been stabbed over fifteen times.'

'Right, back to work!'

Boomed the voice from behind the newspaper. Like the changing of the guard, Mick left the toilet as the not so quiet man entered it. Michael was more than slightly concerned.

'He's blitzed, what are we going to do. If he gets caught? They might breach the three of us.'

'Calm down let's just see what happens.'

'Calm down and end up in the jail. I say we should stick him in before he comes back out of there.'

'You don't do that. You don't stick folk in.'

'But we'll all get it!'

'Only if the cunt notices, he hardly looks out from behind that paper. Just you keep your cool and if he does get caught you never seen anything and for fuck sake leave the talking to me.'

Brian reappeared and the painting continued. Finally with only an hour of the shift to go Colin figured they were home and dry. Suddenly disaster; the Supervisor confronted them. There was a smile on his face and an empty quarter bottle in his hand.

CHAPTER 13 POOR DEFENCELESS WEE WILLIE

It had been a long shift even by Community Service standards. Colin's heart was heavy and his head was fit to burst. Entering the pub his main concern was Mig. Was he still in the one piece and if he was, in view of Brian Something's earlier revelations, did he really want to see him.

First things first if ever there was a time when he needed a pint it was now. Mig bounced up from their usual table and met him at the bar.

'I'll get it.! Two lagers and two Southern Comfort.'

He turned to Colin. 'Hard shift?'

'Wait till I get a pint down me and I'll tell you about it.'

This did not take long.

'When you didn't turn up this morning I thought something had happened to you.'

'It kicked off heavy last night. I had to spend the night at Pamela's. I went home this morning for a change of clothes and the police were waiting for me. I'm just in here in front of you, I've spent most of the day helping them with their enquires.'

'How what happened?'

There followed a detailed account of last nights events. How anticipating them coming, he had waited in the darkness in the flat above. Then team handed they had put in his door and how he had seen them off, hid the gun and cemented his alibi by spending the night at Pamela's. Colin lowered his voice.

'You blew half the whale tail off of the Cossy with a Shotgun. Ha Ha Ha!!.. I guess that'll be pretty much the last word on it then.'

The mad look was in place.

'The last word on it, no fucking way, they done over Wing Nut leaving me without a runner, they threatened me, then they came through my door!'

The big man glared in to space.

'No they haven't heard the last of this, I have plans for Gallagher and you're going to help me.'

Colin sat in silence, drugs, violence, shotguns, the whole thing was getting more and more out of control at an increasingly alarming rate. He just wanted to run away but to where. To the refrigerator that had become home. Home to the awkward questions and the loaded silences at least here in the pub anaesthetic was at hand.

'What about the community service? They might breach you for not turning up this morning.'

'I was helping the police with their enquires. I don't think they can argue with that.'

'How did it go with the police?'

'They were trying to get wide, telling me that they have a witness to the whole thing. To which I replied that's good someone seen my flat getting burgled then I hope you got a statement. Of course that didn't go down too well so next thing they're giving it. 'We found a discharged shotgun cartridge at the scene and are currently dusting it for your fingerprints.' By this point I'm having trouble keeping a straight face. As though I would be that fucking stupid, not me — one shot fired, one used cartridge carefully disposed of down Pamela's toilet.'

'They just let you go?'

'They had nothing to hold me on they're not that smart and it's not as though Gallagher's about to talk to them he's out on borrowed time as it is.'

Pauses for a moment to drink.

'They did a proper search of my flat though everything was all over the place. Anyway what happened at the community service was it a long day without me?

'I'll bet wee Mick and the Daily Record didn't think so.'

Colin grinned. 'The wee man was getting it tight off the Supervisor he was winding him up about going to jail rubber gloves and cavity searches.'

Mig laughed. 'If he ever ends up in the nick his cavity will have more to worry about than rubber gloves. Could you picture it?'

Puts on best gruff tone.

'It's all right Wee Man I'll still respect you in the morning.'

Wee pathetic tone.

'Going to not do that — gonny nooooo...'

After much laughter Colin got up to go to the bar.

'Sit down I'll get them.'

'It's my round.'

'You can get the next one.'

Linda was looking particularly sexy the charming voice came into play.

'You're looking nice.'

These were the seeds that fell upon the stony ground.

'You're not saying much.'

Linda pulled out her coldest smile, the one that generally came in to play at the end of the night to humour drunken customers, the ones who did not seem to understand the meaning of time gentlemen please and who had built up an immunity to don't you people have homes to go to?

'What exactly would I have to say to you? You dropped me the minute that wee slut appeared on the scene. Oh by the way tell Pamela I'm asking for her and the children and I hope her STD's not playing up too badly.'

'I'll have the same again please.'

114

She was talking and Mig liked a challenge the pints were being poured.

'No but how have you been?'

'How have I been? Is this when the pub is quiet or is it when we have wall to wall drunken regulars asking if I'm wearing my black ones tonight.'

He couldn't help himself, he started to laugh.

'That'll be six pounds eighty.'

Mig handed her a tenner with the instruction keep the change she rang up the till and crammed the change into the charity box. Lifting the pints he made his way back to the table surprisingly Linda followed with the half's.

'How's Marion? How many months now?'

'She's fine, about three months.'

Linda smiled. 'Tell her I'm asking for her, I keep meaning to phone her but this place keeps me pretty busy.'

As though to highlight this Ian the Landlord drew her attention to a crowd of fans who had just spilled in after the old firm clash.

'I will.'

Mig took his seat.

'So the Mouth was getting it from the Daily Record then.'

'Never again will the wee man be able to look at a rubber glove in the same way not even to watch his Mammy wash the dishes. Then the Creature it starts rattling on like a budgie on speed he has only downed a quarter bottle of vodka right there and then.'

'Did our man notice?'

'He nearly got away with it but the Daily Record found the empty bottle hidden in the toilet down behind the pan.'

'He would have loved that.'

'That was it, he's giving it — 'if I don't find out who this belongs to you will all get breached one phone call that's all it takes then about two weeks to process the paperwork.' Me, I'm keeping my mouth shut, the wee man he's on the verge of pissing himself and the Creature he smells like a brewery that's on piece work. Give him his due though he stuck his hand up to it.'

'What happened then?'

'The call was made to the social worker to come out and witness it, he was enjoying himself rubbing it right in. The creature he's had enough, says to the Daily Record so I'm going to jail in a couple of weeks so I guess I wouldn't have too much to lose by putting your face in right now.'

Mig smiled in anticipation. 'Please tell me that he done it'

'No gave the bastard a real fright though.'

Colin sipped at his southern comfort, Mig spoke.

'Getting back to the business at hand, we do Gallagher tonight.'

'Will the police not be watching you just now?'

'Fuck them, this is personal and we do it tonight.'

It was the 'we' bit that concerned Colin the most, happily before there was time for Mig to elaborate a distraction arrived in the shape of Dodgey who was looking the worse for ware he came over to their table.

'I'm looking for Wing Nut have you seen him?' He asked.

Mig subtly kicked Colin under the table.

'Last time we seen him was Thursday night what do you want him for.'

The answer to that was visibly obvious Dodgey was rattling.

'I only have a couple of pounds I need some Valium or something.'

The big man looked smug. 'Sit down.'

He lifted his pint and looked into it thoughtfully.

'A couple of pounds would have got you your Valium, that's if I had some, but let's face it wee man, a couple of pounds is not going to get your or something.'

Dodgey was starting to shake there was desperation in his voice.

'I've got a sharp C.D player still in the box two hundred it cost; you can have it for fifty!'

He laughed.

'Wee man right now I could probably have it for a ten pound bag.

Colin's stomach was starting to turn he got to his feet.'

'Time I was going home.'

'Sit on your arse.'

Mig handed Dodgey a tenner.

'Get a round in and when you come back we will discuss a way around your problem.'

Reluctantly Colin sat back down he shouted after Dodgey.

'Nothing for me!'

'Looks like I've just found myself a new runner. Some things take care of themselves other things you have to take care of by yourself. This place closes at twelve I'll get you in here at half eleven.'

'I don't know about this.'

'I didn't hear that. You owe me one for that security guard, remember and you can also think on it as protecting your investment. Half eleven okay. Half eleven okay...'

'Okay. Okay. Half eleven, I'll be here.'

Walking home Colin wondered what Mig had in mind for later but in truth part of him was glad he didn't know. He paused for a moment outside his front door he was home sanctuary for a few hours at least and he was going to make the most of that time to relax. Today had been a long day and by the looks of it, it wasn't over by a long shot.

He opened the door to the homely smell of boil in the bag curry. The hall was in darkness; he closed the front door and reached for the light switch. His hand never quite made it to the switch; unbeknown to Colin in his absence Mary the Man had come round to visit and she had brought her pet dog Wee Willie. The first hint that Colin got of this was when the Yorkshire Nipper successfully ambushed him in the half light. As he reached for the light switch it sank it's teeth into the soft flesh on the back of his leg — hanging on tenaciously; while snarling viciously and shaking it's body from side to side with a ferocity that would have put an angry tiger to shame. Colin screamed in a mixture of surprise and pain causing the Nipper to redouble its efforts. He reached down hoping to grab and throttle it but it had seen that one before. It easily evaded all attempts to grab it while still finding plenty of time to mercilessly punish the hapless fingers.

The living room door opened casting light into the hall now he could see the little fucker. He let loose with a couple of well aimed kicks but he might as well have been moving in slow motion.

'I saw that!' Shrieked Mary the Man.

The Nipper ran behind her wearing it's best cowed expression while continuing to bark furiously.

'Did you see that? Did you see that Marion? The big brute tried to kick Wee Willie.'

Marion scowled. Colin was momentarily stunned by the suddenness of the attack but was not about to take his eyes off of the Nipper who was presently bouncing backwards and forwards, psyching itself up for another go.

'Look at him!' Snarled Mary picking it up.

'The Wee Souls terrified.'

Colin was speechless, the Nipper was at full pitch, Marion was asking where he had been to till this time and the prophet of doom was doing what she did best standing there looking ugly and hoping for an opportunity to make a bad situation worse.

'I went for a couple of pints.'

This was barely heard over the relentless barking of the Nipper but Mary heard it.

'Come home full of drink and start trying to kick a defenceless wee dog.'

He pointed at the Nipper who made an unsuccessful lunge at his finger.

'The fucking thing attacked me the minute I came in the door.'

Mary made great play of being offended by Colin's language.

'My Wee dog wouldn't hurt a fly and I'm sorry Marion but I'm not staying here to take drunken abuse off of him.'

Colin had the urge to grab her and throw her out the door but this would once again involve putting his hands in range of poor defenceless Wee Willie. Mary was right in there.

'I can see now what you've had to put up with all these years, and you in your condition too.'

Colin entered the kitchen.

'There's always room on my couch for you.'

He returned from the kitchen holding a large pot of tepid water that had been used earlier to heat the curries and with great personal satisfaction he threw it about the poisonous one and the still yapping Nipper. He then opened the front door and said only one word.

'Out!!'

CHAPTER 14 GET INTO THE PASSENGER SEAT I'M DRIVING.

Sitting in the back of the Capri Colin was starting to panic he was late for work and Mig was driving in the wrong direction. Despite his best attempts to make this clear he could not be heard. If he didn't get to work soon he would lose his job. He protested again but the car just went faster. In the front passenger seat the Supervisor was giving Mig directions to the prison. There were no doors in the back, he was somehow pinned to the seat and no matter how loud he shouted no one could hear what he was saying.

Ahead in the road he could see Linda, he was shouting to warn them, why couldn't they see her; she was right in front of them? There was a loud thud as the car hit her but Mig just kept on driving as though nothing had happened. Out of the side window he could see Marion, she was heavily pregnant and holding her stomach as though in pain. He shouted and banged on the glass but there was no sound. He was suddenly aware of Mary the man who was sitting next to him. She grabbed him by the balls the pain was excruciating. 'Marion doesn't hear you any more. She only listens to me now.'

The car was going increasingly faster while Marion was rapidly disappearing into the distance and Mary was laughing sadistically. He reached down to try and break her grip suddenly her hand turned into a small mouth with sharp teeth, and started biting into his fingers, he felt the pain, seen the blood, screamed but still could not make a sound.

Colin woke with a start; he was covered in sweat and shaking uncontrollably. It was pitch black — he had lost all sense of time, he reached for Marion but she wasn't there the red glowing numbers on the clock read 23:05. He turned on the bedside light, it was dark, and it was night time.

He got up and made his way down the stairs from the living room. He could hear the sound of the television at the bottom of the stairs he stepped barefoot onto a wet patch of carpet. It was coming back to him it was still Saturday there was still something to be done. That was it, he was to meet Mig in the pub at half past eleven he reached for the living room door handle then it occurred to him that it must be about quarter past already there wasn't time for an argument. He slid quietly back upstairs got dressed quickly before making his way back down and sneaking out the front door.

The Wee Barrel was jumping even for a Saturday night, the old firm clash of the afternoon swelling the numbers and adding to the atmosphere. The game had ended in a draw leaving both factions feeling cheated Colin fought his way to the bar, being careful to avoid big Charlie Moncreif who despite the sign above the bar reading no football colours to be worn was standing there larger than life and twice as loud in his Rangers top knocking them back and making loud noises about just how much the bastards had back handed the Referee and other less subtle comments.

Colin noticed Mig he was sat at the usual table with Dodgey who for his part was looking ten times better than when last he had seen him earlier in the day he ordered a pint and joined them. Conversation was difficult the earlier banter and selective slagging from the rival fans was degenerating in to increasingly louder sectarian chants with more than a hint of underlying malice.

'Make yourself scarce I want to talk to Colin.' Said Mig.

'And remember five to twelve.'

'Five to twelve' Confirmed Dodgey.'

Grinning from ear to ear he got up and made his way to the bar.

'What was that about?'

'You'll see later, in the meantime get that pint down you, it's time we were out of here.'

They left the pub and started to make their way to Mig's flat.

'What have you got in mind?'

Asked Colin, trying to sound keen in an attempt to hide the fact that he was shiting himself.

'First I'm going to change into my steel toe caps and pick something up, we can take it from there.'

'What do you want me to do?'

'That depends, you just do what I tell you to do, when I tell you to do it, and leave the rest to me, we'll suss it when we get there.'

As they got to the close he handed Colin the keys for the Capri.

'You warm up the motor and I'll be back in a couple of minutes.'

Meanwhile back at the Wee Barrel the night was starting to draw to a close. Passions had been running high all day. It was a simple formula; take two rival factions, some deep rooted religious bigotry, hide it behind teams of different colours, mix in several hours of heavy drinking, some serious sarcasm, add a few sectarian songs, light the blue and green touch paper and....retire.

Unseen by all, Dodgey had tipped the contents of the ashtray in to Chas Moncreif's pint. A few seconds later Chas turned to the guy in the Celtic scarf who had obviously been responsible for this and smashed him in the face with the offending ashtray. The touch paper had been well and truly lit — within minutes the whole pub were at it; glasses flying in all directions, a bar stool put through the gantry, tables being overturned, scuffles right left and centre — the police were going to have a busy night.

Mig returned to the Capri he was carrying a dark plastic bag and a long object wrapped in a bin liner. Ten minutes later they arrived in the slum not so far away. They pulled up quietly, a safe distance from the Gallagher residence. Mig got out and approached on foot. Passing the Cosworth he noticed that the rest of the whale tail spoiler had been removed, revealing that the white car had originally been black; 'that would be about right cheapskate bastard, even the Cosworth was a ringer.'

He quietly entered the close — the light was out it was pitch black, just as he had remembered it. Finished in the close his next stop was the Cosworth. Carefully placing the petrol filled bottle under the front wheel, he lit the fuse, when it exploded it blew burning petrol in all directions, effectively setting fire to the underside of the car. Alerted by the sound of the explosion Gallagher came first to the window, then armed with a baseball bat he came rushing out of the close preceded by the two staffies Ronnie and Reggie. In his anger he hadn't noticed that the dogs were not with him.

Moncreif stood on the outside step, waving the bat and cursing at the pitch of his voice as he watched Mig's Capri scream past. Mig's Capri had screamed past unfortunately for Gallagher it had not been Mig who was driving it, this became painfully apparent when the barrel of the shotgun smashed into his shins dropping him on to his knees and face first down the outside stairs.

Inside the flat door slammed loudly quickly followed by the sounds of the deadbolts being rammed into place a testimony to self preservation.

Outside on the ground Gallagher writhed around in pain clutching at his shins. While preparing for this moment. Mig had put a lot of thought into what he was going to say but caught up in the excitement, he opted instead to repeatedly kick him about the face and body.

Finally satisfied, he walked back to the Capri which had now returned and instructed Colin to…..

'Get into the passenger seat I'm driving.'

This was a request that did not need repeating, and very soon they were on their way.

'I done the bastard, there's no way he is coming back from that.'

'You made a nice job of his motor.'

'That's a warning to other folk out there. I'm the man now, anybody who tries to fuck with me will know what to expect.'

Mig drove the car to a spot just outside the town; a small lay by infamous for fly tipping.

Colin was curious. 'What are we doing here?'

I'm not risking taking this home tonight.'

He wrapped the gun in the bin liner and hid it under a pile of black bin bags that had been left by the side of the road.

'What happened to the dogs?'

'I figured the little bastards would come flying out the minute the door was opened so I scattered a big box of drawing pins all over the close.'

Much to Colin's relief, he had made it home without seeing the inside of a Police Station, this was the upside, the downside was that he had been missed — the spare quilt and pillow laid out on the settee was testimony to this it also warned of what was to come.

'Where were you last night?' That would be the question accompanied by the lie detector stare. Plagued by this and multiple other worries sleep at best was little more than an optimistic notion. The quarter bottle of vodka in the fridge that he had bought Marion the week before, maybe it would help. Vodka was not his weapon of choice, it wasn't even a drink that he would normally thank you for, especially when there was nothing to put in it but this was an emergency. His face contorted as the alcohol burned it's way down his throat — like the rest of the day had been hard and bitter.

The settee was uncomfortable and the night was long. As the light started to come up he put off going to the toilet, as this would involve passing the bedroom door, revealing his presence and inviting the conflict that would come soon enough. As though summoned by this very thought he could hear Marion coming down the stairs every step getting louder like the approaching giant giving it 'FEE FIE FOE FUM...' The only difference was this was all too real. Despite burning bladder and bursting head it was time to hide under the quilt and feign deep sleep.

Marion entered the living room. 'Oh, so you're back are you?'

No reply no sign of consciousness.

'You can lie there pretending to be asleep just now, but don't think we're not going to be talking about this later!'

She went into the kitchen and started to fill the kettle Colin was bursting for a pee and the sound of the running water wasn't helping. The burning bladder had been distracting from the bursting head — this was to be short lived as Marion started up the washing machine, then proceeded to wash the previous night's dishes — slamming plates mugs and cutlery down onto the stainless steel draining board to resounding effect. Colin's nerves were totally on edge each sound like a hammer blow to the head. He found himself thinking that this must have been what it was like for those poor buggers during the war, hiding in the trenches, waiting for the next explosion, too frightened to put their heads up for fear of losing them.

Tension was growing, the Hotpoint Logic 800 was working it's self up for the spin cycle, and Marion, in a fit of truly inspired sadism, was plugging in the Hoover. His vodka fuelled imagination suddenly took him to the gates of Hell, where he was banging away furiously and screaming 'Let me in' but no such mercy was to be had — as simultaneously the Hotpoint hit the spin cycle and the Hoover burst in to life. He pulled the quilt tighter over his head marvelling at her tactics, this was a mistake, a movement, a sign of consciousness.The cover was suddenly pulled back adding the unbearable glare of the electric light to his other torments he shielded his eyes.

'Would you like a cup of tea?' Her voice was soft.

'That would be great love.'

Marion's voice suddenly hit a pitch that fell just short of breaking the windows.

'The kettle's just boiled get me one while you're at it!!!'

Colin groaned.

'Then you can tell me where you were last night?'

He pulled the quilt back over his head; she was having none of this and pulled it back down.

'Then we can discuss where you're going to stay tonight.'

Realising he was beat and after making a much needed trip to the bathroom, he entered the kitchen. Maybe there was an opportunity to escape from the War zone.

'We've ran out of Tea bags, I'll nip round and get some.'

'Oh no you don't! That's the last couple of Sunday's you've pulled the disappearing act, but it's not going to happen today! I'll go to the shops.'

There was no arguing with that face, but at least she had turned the Hoover off. The minute Marion left he turned off the washing machine and the light then crawled back under the quilt. She returned in what seemed like a very short time made him a cup of tea and was almost friendly. Normally he would have sussed it but the hangover had taken the edge off of his judgment.

'So where did you go last night?'

This was a loaded question, time for a plausible lie.

'When I woke up I went back round to the pub.'

Marion was half smiling.

'Right enough, where else would you go?'

'It was busier than usual, what with the game and that.'

'Meet anybody?'

'No, I just sat and had a few myself.'

'No doubt you stayed till the death.'

'You know me, I was one of the last to leave.'

Her mood suddenly changed and not for the better.

'So you went back to the pub, you never met anybody, and you were one of the last to leave.'

Instinctively Colin became defensive.

'Look, I went to the pub and had a few pints. That's all.'

'No Colin, that's not all.' Her voice was starting to rise.

'The girl from the paper shop is just after telling me that there was a real barny in that place last night, over a dozen people arrested.'

He was well and truly rumbled. Her voice was demanding.

'So where were you?'

He was on the spot and speechless.

'Where were you, I'm waiting.'

'I was at Mig's place.'

'And I'm the Pope's aunty.'

Marion looked hurt.

'I didn't want to believe it but Mary was right. I'm five minutes pregnant, and you've already got yourself a bit on the side.'

The thought of having a bit on the side flattered Colin's ego, this had the horrific side effect of showing in his face as a half smile.

'I don't have a bit on the side. '

'Don't you lie to me Colin Spears that look on your face gives you away every time.'

Colin was trying his hardest to look serious, adding all the more to his obvious guilt.

'I should have known better than to have gotten pregnant.'

'Don't say that.'

'It's true.'

Disaster the strong angry woman bawling and shouting at him he could just about cope with, but she had started to cry. He tried to cuddle her but she pushed him away and turned her back. She composed herself.

'Just you go away and do whatever it is that you want to do.'

Colin pulled her head onto his chest, her tears had stuck her long hair to her face and were seeping through his clothes, this time his voice really was sincere.

'There isn't anyone else.'

Time for a logical argument.

'Think about it, nothing happens around here without Mary getting wind of it, if there was someone else she would have been bursting down the door to quote you name age and natural hair colour.'

'I suppose your right.'

'Everything's going to be all right.'

CHAPTER 15   THE POISON DWARF.

Last night they had managed to talk to each other, a rare occurrence over the last couple of weeks. A cosy night in, a take away curry, a carry out even the video they had hired in had been passable. Domestic harmony at its most recent best, but as usual after Sunday night all too soon comes Monday morning, the chill in the air and always less time than you really need. Just to add to this Colin found himself in the corner shop waiting to buy of all things a packet of Caramel Wafers, a pregnant woman craving, don't try and understand it, just go and get it, and what about Mig the phone call.

'Are you coming out for a pint?'

'Not tonight.'

'Oh, so your Mammy's not letting you out to play then.'

'Cheeky bastard', after the events of the weekend Colin figured all debts were paid in full and he intended to see a whole lot less of Mig and try to get his life back to some form of normality. It suddenly occurred to him that he had been standing in the queue just a little too long. He still had to get back with the Caramel Wafers before he could make his way to work.

Going in late on Monday morning after being off on Friday would not be a good idea. The conversation between the woman in front of him and the shop assistant who was serving had already covered the weather, the best deals, her down the road and had moved on to travelling hairdressers.

'Ten pounds, ten pounds for that. I'm telling you, my daughter would have made a better job of it, it's not even my usual colour.'

'No, no it's definitely not.'

'No, you know me I'm usually more kind of subtle.'

Colin's attention was split between the peroxide holocaust and the animal print coat. Subtle as an overflowing ash tray— mutton dressed as leopard. His patience was wearing thin.

'Any chance of getting served here?'

'When I'm finished serving the customer in front of you.'

Resume conversation.

'Don't get me wrong, our Isa got her and she was delighted.'

'Maybe she would get it right the next time, now that she knows you.'

Sceptical shake of the head tactical look at the finger nails.

'No I don't know if I would have her again.'

Patience was one thing but this was bordering on taking the piss.

'Some of us have work to go to.'

'And some of us are already at our work.'

Came the acid blue rinsed reply, as the Caramel Wafers were rang up as slowly and reluctantly as possible. Colin turned to leave.

'The young ones these days, they don't know the meaning of the word work!'

'Oh, your dead right Effie, they have it far too easy, not like it was in our day.'

Colin bit his tongue, even if there had been time to argue there would have been no point. Caramel Wafers delivered he half walked half ran to Murphy's, as he got there the night shift were spilling out across the car park, this was not a good sign.

He was met by the Boyle brothers. Three brothers, a sister, a father and a few cousins worked there the uncle was a hirer and firer. Nepotism so blatant that the Gaffer Fogarty would joke he had been sent down a plague of Boyles.

'Did you hear about the accident?'

It was Andy the eldest of the brothers who spoke, Colin shook his head.

'It happened on Friday afternoon, McKenzie had had a couple in the pub at dinner time, smoked a joint when he got back, then he ran over Wee Janice from the office with the forklift.'

Colin's heart sank; he had sold him the blow the day before.

'Was she badly hurt?' He asked, not sure that he really wanted to know.

'Squashed her foot and broke her leg, fuck me she screamed so loud you could hear her over the machines, there was blood everywhere, her foot popped like a grape.'

These were details that Colin could have done without hearing, the optimism that he had woken up with had been replaced by feelings of sickness and panic, and it wasn't getting any better.

'The Health and Safety were in within the hour, threatening to shut the place.'

'I better get in.'

'You're late already.'

Said James, the middle brother with a grin that he wasn't trying to hide.

'Watch yourself!' Warned Andy as Colin walked away.

'The Management are asking all sorts of awkward questions.'

Colin stamped his clock card, it was four minutes past eight, funny rule that you could get away with being three minutes late but not four. He ran round the outside of the factory and entered by the back door, to give the impression that he had just come from the smoke room, a ploy that had been known to work in the past, but not this morning. Fogerty the Gaffer was hard but fair, but the look on his face read like a newspaper headline.

'You're late, and The Poison Dwarf wants to see you.'

Fogarty was making reference to the works manager Macfarlane a man who compensated for his lack of inches by being an unreasonable bastard.

Colin knocked on the door of his Office. Finally invited in he was made to wait a full five minutes while the bastard pretended to be engrossed in his paperwork.

'Mr Spears, off on Friday and late this morning.'

He was enjoying himself and paused a moment for best effect.

'Quite frankly Colin, here at Murphy's Packaging we are not impressed by that kind of attitude.'

Macfarlane was looking him up and down. The phone rang and there was a further five minute delay while Macfarlane growled down the line to whoever was unfortunate enough to be on the other side. He slammed down the receiver.

'Off on Friday, late this morning, and to my knowledge you have never worked overtime since you started here.'

At Murphy's you didn't get to work a Sunday at double time if you didn't work the Saturday, and Colin was not about to make the Bastards day by explaining why he couldn't work on a Saturday. He kept his mouth shut.

'So what have you got to say for yourself?'

Intense stare. Colin knew what was coming and wasn't about to start grovelling on what was already a lost cause. Macfarlane was disappointed by this.

'I'm waiting.'

'Okay, I was off, I was late, if you're going to pay me off just do it.'

'Oh it's not quite as simple as that Colin, there was an accident on the shop floor on Friday afternoon, we suspect that drugs were involved and we got a wee hint that you might know something about it.'

Colin was starting to panic but knew he had to bluff it.

'I wasn't even here on Friday, and I don't know anything about any drugs.'

'I hope for your sake you're telling the truth, because there are close circuit cameras in every department in here. All we have to do is look over the tapes then it would be a matter for the police.'

If this was a bluff it was a fucking good one. Colin tried to act normal Macfarlane continued.

'Anyway in the meantime Murphy's no longer have need of your services. Your weeks lying time and any holiday pay you are due will

131

be paid into your bank this week, shut the door on the way out.'

If it had not been for the fact that an assault charge would have guaranteed him a jail sentence, he would have punched the smug little bastard's lights out on the spot. He was tempted to slam the door on his way out but decided that if he left it open it would have better effect.

He walked past Fogarty on the way out; there was no need for words. Crossing the car park Macfarlane's words were still ringing in his head.

'At Murphy's packaging we are not impressed with that type of attitude.'

Well, he had never been too impressed with three pound fifty an hour.

'Shut the door on your way out.'

If he had known where the bastard lived, he could have taken the big man round and shown him some attitude, he wouldn't be quite so self assured with a couple of broken legs. The bit about the camera's he wasn't so sure about. It could be an angle after all if the accident could be blamed on McKenzie being under the influence, then the fact that the girl should never have been on the shop floor without protective footwear might be slightly overlooked.

It was still a worry though, what if he had been caught on camera selling. No he couldn't afford to start thinking like that, and the wee girl what about her, Andy Boyle's words came back to haunt him. 'There was blood everywhere, her foot popped like a grape.' He cringed. 'She screamed so loud you could hear her over the machines.'

He clutched at his forehead, what had he done? His conscience fought with it's self. Okay he had sold McKenzie the blow, but he hadn't expected the idiot to smoke it while he was working. He couldn't even console himself with that one — he had seen him do it before, out in the yard.

Paid off, possibly caught on camera selling, at least partly responsible for a horrific accident and now home to give Marion the bad news. Was there any upside to anything anymore? He looked back at the ugly soulless factory that he would never return to; he smiled maybe just a wee bit.

Marion was up when he got back.

'You're back early, what happened?'

'I got bumped for my time keeping.'

'What did they say?'

He gave her the edited version.

'The Prophet of doom was right, bad time keepers and folk who wouldn't do overtime first. She'll be so happy when she finds out she was right.'

'You were too good for that place anyway. You only took that job because your trial was coming up, it served it's purpose, it helped keep you out of jail.'

Jail, his stomach jumped at the very sound of the word. Marion was reassuring.

'Try not to worry about it, I'll get you a cup of tea and something to eat, then maybe we could jump the bus down town and do some shopping.'

Two hours later walking through the shopping mall, Marion tugged at Colin's arm.

'There's that guy!'

'What guy?'

She subtly drew his attention to a man being pushed in a wheelchair, both arms were in plaster and he had a bandage around his head, he was being pushed by a woman roughly the same age, two small girls walked beside him.

Marion continued. 'I'm sure it's him. The security guard that gave evidence at your trial.'

'No it's just someone who looks like him.'

Telling lies to his wife was not something that He was good at, he could feel his face going red.

'I'll be back in a minute, call of nature.'

Colin took off in the direction of the public toilets, he had barely made it to the cubicle before being quickly reminded of what he had had for breakfast. He rejoined Marion about ten minutes later she was still talking about it.

'I'm sure that was him, he looked like he had been run over by a car or something.'

The thought occurred to Him that the poor bastard would probably have gotten off lighter if he had been. The sight of the wife and children ripped right into his already heaving conscience.

'Maybe it was him.'

Further down the mall a crowd had gathered, there was some sort of commotion going on. Drawn by curiosity they joined the crowd to get a better view.

Two of the mall security were struggling to restrain a young man who was kicking and shouting. Colin recognised him, it was Hodgey.

'What did he do?' Asked Marion.

An elderly lady in the crowd volunteered an answer.

'We were sitting in the cafe, when that wee yob came running in and tried to steal the charity box.'

'Just as well the security guards were here.'

'The security weren't here, it was two women in the queue that grabbed him and held him till they got here, probably a drug addict.'

'A charity box, how desperate can you get.'

Marion commented, as the desperate one was being frog marched away, still struggling and protesting his innocence at the pitch of his voice; Colin looked on and shook his head. Some more shopping and a pub lunch later, they were back home in the living room, Marion gazed out of the window into the garden.

'You know what would look nice out there? One of those Rhodie thing thing bushes.'

'Rhododendron.' Corrected Colin.

'The ones with the big purple blooms there's something romantic about them I've always liked them, I've always wanted to be able to look out of the window and see one.'

'Maybe when the weather gets better.'

She smiled. 'I'll hold you to that.'

Her attention was drawn to a car that had just pulled up outside.

'There's a car just pulled up and two guys wearing suites are coming up the path.'

Colin had a look.

'They're probably selling double glazing or something, I'll give them short shift.'

He opened the door just in time to see the uniform back up getting out of the marked car. The double glazing salesmen had come complete with a search warrant.

CHAPTER 16 TEN TO ONE ON ILLEGAL SUBSTANCE

The Police had come and gone, and so had Marion. Shock was setting in, it had all happened so quickly they had waltzed in waved a warrant and turned the place over, and even as they were explaining that even though they hadn't found anything, it was part of an ongoing inquiry she was throwing things into a bag. Marion was gone. The warm cosy home of the night before had become a vacant space.

He opened his third can of lager and swallowed almost half, usually he preferred to drink from a glass. What was the fucking difference, she was gone. Okay but to where? Mary the Man's?

Mary the Man, gossip and shit stirrer extraordinaire, no she would be the last person that Marion would want to know she had just had her house searched by the drug squad. If Mary got wind of it, it would be all over the scheme within the hour.

More likely she would have gone round to her younger sister's place. Shirley the one that lived in the Brat estate, whose man Tony, or as he preferred these days Anton was without doubt the most pretentious wanker you could ever have the misfortune to be related to. A guy so shallow he probably wore a shirt and tie in bed at night. Shirley he could take, even though she had knocked him back that time he had tried to feel her up in the kitchen at the Christmas family get together. Shirley he could take, our man Anton that was another matter. If he wasn't trying to sell you an insurance policy he was gassing on about the size of his mortgage, preferably at full volume, in the pub on his mobile. Colin had often marvelled that someone with so much debt could manage to have so big an ego.

There would be no point in going round there now she would need a couple of days to cool down then if he was really lucky she might come back. He eyed his reflection in the dead T.V. screen it was dark and distorted. Yeah. The empty can bounced off of the wall the mood swing had landed on anger. Somebody had caused this somebody had sent the police to his door it had to have been that prick Macfarlane from Murphy's.

Colin was aware of a spontaneous pounding in his right temple. That would be about right it wasn't enough to pay him off, no let's just send round the police; well the bastard was going to regret that in a big way.

Time to phone a friend. Frustration was rising.

Mig's home number was ringing out and his mobile was going straight to voice mail. Knowing Mig he would either be with the Sweaty Palm working up a thirst or in the Wee Barrel quenching one. Colin decided to make for the pub, lifeless dive that it was, it would be preferable to sitting there alone in the accusing emptiness.

Walking down the street he was more than aware of the eyes behind the curtains and the looks from passers by he had an overpowering urge to scream ' the bastards never found anything' he restrained himself even if he did get a chance to explain who would want to hear it. Folk around there were for the most part on the dole with nothing going on in their lives.

To them scandal was always preferable to the truth anyway he didn't give a fuck what they thought, unfortunately though, Marion did. Two overly large women were approaching on the opposite side of the street giving accusing looks and stage whispers.

'I'm telling you Effie, four police cars, three marked ones and one C.I.D. well you can tell can't you.'

The mouthy slag he recognised from somewhere the ball face, fake tan and vulgar abundance of gold jewellery were familiar but it was the burnt out bottle blond hair sticking out in all directions that jogged his memory. It was her, the ignorant slapper that had caused him to be late for his work this morning. It was none other than the peroxide holocaust.

'You're right there Morag the unmarked one that would have been the drug squad.'

More accusing looks. 'The young ones, they're bringing the area right down.'

Colin had heard enough.

'Listen Torag, why don't you just go and take a running fuck to yourself you dried up old Gorgon!'

Walking on Colin's back was to the exaggerated performances of mock horror and competing snarls. Something about 'getting her man' and something about 'get your facts straight I'm not a Mormon I'm a Catholic.'

Here it was again the Wee Barrel another place that time had forgot. Old Willie Moffat perched in his usual corner staring at his half through his national health milk bottle bottoms as much a permanent fixture as the nicotine laden cobweb hanging from the light shade. The only recent change being the broken mirror behind the optic measures a visual testimony to the warmth and sporting goodwill that generally surrounds an old firm clash.

Colin ordered a pint. Mig was there he was sitting with Pamela and her side kick she's Margaret. Big Caroline who was serving either didn't know that all action Margaret had been barred for head butting the Landlord or she was pretending not to know to avoid the obvious dangers that might be involved in asking her to leave.

'I'll get that and the same again for the ladies.'

Mig slapped a twenty pound note onto the bar.

'Back in a minute the karsi calls.'

Who was Colin to argue he had a quick squint at the ladies barely tea time on Monday and the Sweaty Palm was dressed for a Saturday night on the town. She had over done it with the eye make up though and in the dingy half light examining her polished nails she actual did look like a vampire. She's Margaret appeared to have had her eye brow pierced since last he had seen her, this was not an improvement.

'Has the big man won the lottery?'

Inquired Caroline, as she poured the pints; another lager for Mig and a Guinness for Margaret.

'It's just that in the last hour or so he's fed at least fifty quid into the fruit machine and jukebox and he's been keeping the Terra Hawks there going on drink and fags.'

Colin made the effort and smiled.

'I heard he done all right at the bookies over the weekend.'

A seasoned barmaid with twelve years of working in the same scheme pub was a wee bit smarter than that.

'Ten to one on illegal substance'

She muttered to herself as she turned to the optics to pour Pamela's Bacardi.

Mig returned. 'So what's the script?'

Mig was beaming all over his face a man very aware of his standing and enjoying the decadence of having too much money to spend. Caroline retreated to the far end of the bar and started polishing the glasses.

'I got paid off from my work.'
Mig grinned.

'There's plenty of easy money to be made without answering to arseholes.'

To emphasise this he pulled out a wad that would have choked a horse.

'The police busted my house.'

The wad was quickly returned to the pocket. The Sweaty Palm was starting to feel neglected. Well it had been about five minutes and Mig was committing the ultimate crime he was talking to someone else. Gliding up to the bar preceded by a heavy air of perfume and cigarette smoke she slid her self between them her back to Colin totally ignoring his existence as was her custom with lesser beings which was quite a trick considering she had almost skewered his foot with a stiletto heel. She started to kiss Mig passionately Colin tried hard not to throw up. She whispered into Mig's ear.

'It's getting lonely over there.'

He broke their embrace.

'You take the drinks; I'll be over in a minute.'

Pamela picked up the drinks and turned away.

'Don't be too long.'

Her voice had all the charm of a spoiled child Mig ignored her there was business to be discussed.

'When?'

'About an hour ago.'

'Did they find anything?'

'I'm still walking about aren't I.'

Mig swallowed some of his pint.

'Some cunt's stuck you in.'

Colin lowered his voice and related the events of the morning of how he had been paid off with threats of video footage. Mig was not convinced.

'If they really had something on video they would just have came and taken you away.'

In his anger Colin had not considered this. Mig continued.

'No, it would have been somebody else. somebody a bit closer to home.'

Colin's mind went blank. Pamela appeared again, she slid between them rubbing herself against Mig.

'I'll need to be going soon.'

It was the full sugar coated tone backed up by the subtle hand sliding up and down Mig's groin. This was normally an offer that could not be refused but Mig had had her twice already today he gently pushed her to one side.

'If you have to go you have to go, I'll see you later.'

Pamela did not take rejection well.

'If you're lucky you might.' She snarled.

Stirred into action by her friends change in tone and the sudden realisation that of the nine or ten glasses on the table all were empty She's Margret came lumbering towards the bar. Colin cringed but much to his relief and surprise she put an arm round Pamela escorting her towards the door.

'Come on hen it's time we were up the road.'

The ladies gone Colin and Mig took a seat and conversation resumed.

'No it wouldn't have been them from your work.'

Mig looked thoughtful.

'I know I told you not to but did you give anybody tic, because tic is a bit hard to collect if your in the nick, know what I mean.'

'I never gave tic and I can't think of anyone with a grudge. What about Gallagher and his mob.'

Mig shook his head.

'They don't know you besides they're like me they don't involve the police they deal with their own problems, credibility and all that.'

Another round was ordered.

'Talking about credibility we need to find out who it was and deal with it.'

For once Colin was in full agreement.

'I'm well up for that, the fact they didn't find any thing didn't stop my wife leaving.'

The round appeared and was paid for. Mig had noticed that the drink was starting to get the better of Colin.

'That was a bit heavy getting your house busted but at least they never found your stash.'

'No, I had re papered the wall thank fuck.'

Mig smiled to himself.

'Get that drink down you there's somebody out there due a good slap and we have to work out who and take care of it because we're in charge now and no cunt is going to fuck with us.'

'I'll drink to that.'

Colin raised his glass anger was the only thing keeping him awake. He went to the gents by the time he returned Mig was sitting with Dodgey money and substances had already changed hands. Mig offered to buy Dodgey a pint, totally out of character he refused saying that Hodgey was waiting for him outside.

'I seen him this morning he was being taken away by the mall security for trying to lift a charity box.'

'Lifted this morning and out for tea time.' Reflected Mig.

'I would like to know how he pulled that one. Maybe you should ask him to come in and explain it to me.'

Dodgey's face rapidly changed colours. Mig was getting impatient.

'Get him in here I want to talk to him!'

Dodgey got to his feet and left the pub. He returned a few minutes later with Hodgey in tow. Hodgey was looking more than slightly spaced out.

'Sit him down before he falls down.' Ordered Mig.

'So my man here tells me you got lifted this morning.'

Hodgey burst into a fit of giggles.

'Was that this morning? I think it was.'

More giggles.

'Down at the mall. You should have seen it I bit one of them on the hand.'

He was helpless with laughter and gasping for breath.

'Then, then, the police came and read me my rights.'

He was off again. Mig smiled.

'They do that, don't they, read you your rights.'

He swirled the remains of his pint around the bottom of his glass playfully before draining it.

'Course if you got lifted this morning the only way you would be out by the afternoon would be if you stuck someone else in.'

Colin had just sussed it. Dodgey's arse tightened as he looked on at his friend who was looking to have about as much chance as a rabbit caught in the headlights of an oncoming truck.

'Come here to I tell you something.'

Mig leaned across the table towards Hodgey.

'You just grassed up the wrong folk.'

So saying he smashed the pint glass over Hodge's head and drew the broken remains down his face. Hodgey jumped to his feet overturning his chair he clutched at his face. In his panic to escape he tripped over the downed chair giving Mig just enough time to get round the table and lay in with the boot.

Having caught an elbow in the face the first time Colin managed to pull Mig off on the second attempt as Dodgey quickly scrambled the body to it's feet and out the door.

'The police have been called!' Shouted Caroline from behind the bar.

'So you saw this guy go for me then.'

Stated Mig trying to regain his breath.

'I never seen anything.'

'Yeah.. and you would do well to remember that.'

He warned making for the door Colin closely behind.

CHAPTER 17 I HAVE SOMETHING SHOW YOU

Although unwanted consciousness was still there Colin lay there gripped with fear unable to shake the images of blood and broken glass. He heard a noise someone was in the house was it the police coming for him? Maybe if he lay really still they wouldn't find him the noise continued someone was coming up the stairs he cowered in his hiding place under the bed. Footsteps lights on found.

'What the hell are you doing under there?'

It was Marion, was he relieved? He wasn't sure. He came out and got to his feet shielding his eyes against the light.

'What were you doing hiding under there, you're losing it Colin.'

Her head shook from side to side as she spoke. Colin figured it would be safer not to say 'Actually dear I'm expecting a second visit from the police' He hid behind a blank expression.

'Are you all right?'

The light stung his eyes. 'I'll be all right in a minute.'

'You're some man!'

Marion was still shaking her head.

'Anyway now that it's dark I thought I would come round and pick up a few things. I'll be staying at Shirley's for a couple of day's just until I can work something out with the council and I'm not wanting you worrying about me and the baby, we'll be alright on our own.'

Colin was speechless she never failed to amaze him and as for the baby, the wee fucker wasn't even here yet and already it was jockeying for position. The Tasmanian Devil alarm clock on the dressing table was gently put into a holdall.

'You can't take that.' Protested Colin.

'Oh, can I not? My mother bought that.'

'About the only time the stingy old cow put her hand in her pocket in living memory.'

144

'Don't you slag off my mother your own family is nothing to write home about your father is only ever out of the pub if it's to go to the bookies and that mother of yours huh. You can choose your friends.'

Colin was not about to leave this unanswered. 'What about?'

Tactical problem his mouth was spouting it quicker than his brain was composing it. 'What about?'

'Don't you raise your voice to me Colin Spears!'

A moments gap in the argument, Mischievous silence whoever got in first would have the edge. Too late already she was in there and talk about rapid fire.

'Don't you raise your voice to me.'

'Just don't you even think about it.'

'I'm in here keeping the house.'

'And me, in my condition.'

'And you.'

'You.'

'You're out there losing your job.'

'Getting into all sorts of trouble.'

'Hanging around with all the nutters of the day.'

'Coming home pissed.'

'The police busting the house.'

'Just where do you think this is going.'

She paused to draw breath, thank fuck for small mercies. Then she got that look in her eye the look that says throw away your optimism guard your ghoulies.

'ARE YOU LISTENING TO ME!!!!'

The windows didn't break but it must have been close.

'ARE YOU LISTENING!!!'

Defence mechanism, try sarcasm.

'Do I have an option?'

The option came in the shape of the clock as it flew across the room narrowly missing his head and shattering against the wall. Colin had never liked that clock anyway. He made the mistake of mentioning this. As he went down the back of his head hit the dressing table. What a punch. He came round to a damp cloth on his brow.

'Colin are you alright, I didn't mean it'.

The whole side of his face was in agony not too bad for someone who didn't mean it. For some reason he looked at his watch. It was only quarter past nine how could so much crap have happened in one day. The gesture of looking at his watch was interpreted as 'are the pubs still open.'

'You're alright.'

There was a snarl in her tone. As Marion got to her feet she accidentally stood on his fingers an action which despite causing a loud cry of pain obviously didn't warrant an apology. Colin clutched the throbbing digits with his other hand the crushed fingers had not actually recovered since the Nipper incident the pain was excruciating. Alright! Alright! He had never been less alright in his whole fucking life.

There was no more talk just the packing of the bag. The deliberating over now undisputed bits and pieces. The whole thing taking just a little too long like maybe she was waiting for an explanation or was wanting talked out of going, either way Colin did not have the strength left to get into it. The door closed quietly as she left. He set about the pointless exercise of trying to sleep the violent images of earlier guaranteeing that this would not be happening.

Three days; no sleep, unable to eat, no word from Marion and enough daytime television to insult the intelligence of an earth worm — breaking point was close at hand. So round it was to Shirley and Anton's to the brat estate, the wee poky side door with the bog standard twelve foot by three foot patch of grass at the front. And there it was, Anton's motor, a Ford Fiesta Popular so fucking basic even the paint job looked like it had been finished in primer, not to worry though it had this years letter on the plate. Because let's face it when you lived in a place like this it was important to send out the right message to the neighbours. Anton answered the door, tie perfectly tied, white shirt radiant and the sleeves rolled up, obviously some sort of macho gesture, hands out in front all assertive.

'Colin!'

'Tony!'

'She doesn't want to see you Colin.'

'Get her out here I want to speak to her.'

'She doesn't want to see you Colin so why don't you just clear off, we don't want a scene.'

Aware that his next doors neighbour was watering his token couple of yards of grass. Anton was adopting his bestist, poshist tone. Colin had also noticed the neighbour.

'Just clear off, it wasn't that when you were trying to scrape together the deposit for this fucking egg box.'

A smirk spread across the neighbour's face as he pretended to pull a few imaginary weeds. Anton looked slightly flushed.

'She disnae want tae see yae Colin'.

Anton secretly cursed he had let his language slip. Colin squinted over at the neighbour and raised his voice.

'No you weren't so particular then were you it didn't matter to you that it was stolen money.'

The neighbour was listening intently. Anton leaned forward and whispered through clenched teeth.

'For fuck sake keep your voice down.'

'There's no need for that kind of talk.'

Anton's true colours were rapidly coming to the surface.

'Just get Marion out here, we don't want a scene remember.'

Colin's patience was rapidly wearing thin.

'If she's not out here in two minutes I'm coming in there to get her.'

Marion appeared in the doorway.

'I'll speak to him.'

To avoid further embarrassment and damage to his imagined standing and reputation Anton quickly invited Colin in. The living room was cramped two, two-seater settee's a coffee table in the middle and just enough room for the T.V. Colin and Marion faced each other. Anton diplomatically retreated to the kitchen and Shirley sat on the couch pretending to be interested, the bulk of her attention focused on the Telly and the fascinating goings on in Brookside. Marion spoke first.

'We don't want to be discussing our business here let's go for a walk.'

Five minutes out and they were coming to the outskirts of the Brat estate.

'What's Shirley's wee bit called?' Asked Colin.

'Peacock Gardens.'

He looked back to the rows of identical houses four to a block the builders had been so economic with the ground space it suddenly hit him.

'But none of them really have gardens.'

They continued to walk there was an awkwardness almost like a first date both of them making small talk for fear that the real issues would cause further eruptions.

'Our Anton, I think he has been taking Yuppie lessons.'
'Give them a break they're only trying to better themselves.'

'I suppose.'

'Mind you in the last three day's I have heard enough about insurance policies mortgages and interest rates to last me a life time, I'm surprised Shirley hasn't climbed the walls with boredom.'

'He always was heavy going, even before they got that house we would be sitting in the pub with them when it was his round everybody would be sitting with an empty glass and he would be sitting with a half inch out of his pint prattling on it was embarrassing.'

'He hasn't changed every time I got sugar in my tea I could have swore he was counting the grains.'

The mood had lightened, as they walked past the old church Marion pointed to the bushes not yet in bloom.

'Look Rhodie thing things.'

Colin looked at the bushes they didn't look much without the flowers.

'Do you still want one for the garden?'

Marion didn't answer this instead she opened her handbag and fumbled inside.

'I have something to show you.'

She handed him a small black and white printed picture.

'I was at the hospital getting an ultra sound.'

Pointing to the centre of the picture.

'That's your son or daughter.'

CHAPTER 18 THE PHANTOM MENACE.

February had become March but no one had told the weather. Colin shivered as he slipped out of his trainers and donned the cold uncomfortable work boots. He had a sudden image of the nasty evil little goblin who had engineered the pointless frustration that was community service an aggressive little pen pusher with a bald head glasses and a potency problem no doubt on around fifty grand a year and currently on holiday in warm parts sitting by a pool and laughing into his Gee and Tee.

Mig appeared closely followed by Mick the Mouth who if possible looked even taller and skinnier than last week. Young Michael was trying his best to blend in with the scenery. Colin likewise had no urge to speak to Mig the last time he had seen him was on Monday when he had cut up Hodgey.

Mig though was Mig and being ignored was not on his agenda and let's face it the Daily Record was always fair game.

'Shite, Shite, Shite, Shite, Shite, Shite…. SHITE!!!!'

'What's your problem McGuire?'

'What's my problem, what's my problem? I'll tell you what my problem is I'm right handed and this is a left handed brush!'

For a second or two the Supervisor looked confused, never had points been scored so easily.

'Get on with it and less of your crap.'

The Supervisor was fighting a losing battle with a hangover and wished that he was anywhere else. He turned and walked away.

'You're my witness Colin a right handed man being forced to use a left handed brush. The health and safety are going to hear about this.'

A young boy suddenly appeared he wore shiny black trainers and a bright red face.

'Is this where you do the community service?'

He asked in a pretty shaky voice.

Mig smiled, fresh victims were always welcome. Mick the Mouth was well pleased too not only had he just moved up the food chain but there was history between him and the new arrival and he had something juicy on him. Michael had been in the year above him in school. Greeted by the Supervisor he was taken in to the Office.

Re-appearing ten minutes later wearing standard issue work boots and overalls at least three sizes too big. He pretended not to recognize Mick and took up position between Mig and Colin.

'What did you get your hours for Wee Man?'

Inquired Mig in the most innocent tone he could muster.

'I don't want to talk about it.'

Answered the newcomer to the wall he was painting.

'Oooooh, he doesn't want to talk about it. What do you reckon Colin hit man for the Mafia?'

Mig was giving it his best I'm sizing you up look.

'Hitting on the pick and mix in Woolworth s maybe.'

There was an over exaggerated laugh from wee Mick for once not the target of Mig's untamed wit. The new arrival cringed, just at that moment an unholy stench hit the air and he was given a few more feet of space.

Mick held his nose and pointed accusingly.

'You're reeking!'

'It wasn't me.'

He cried adding all the more to his obvious guilt. Mig was right in there.

'Watch yourselves boys we have in our midst a deadly exponent of the silent controlled fart there is no telling just what else this Phantom Menace might be capable of.'

The Phantom Menace hit an even deeper shade of red.

'You're not here for a carry on, get those walls painted.'

Shouted the Supervisor squinting out from behind his Daily Record.

'Who rattled his cage?' Said Mig just loud enough to be heard.

'Don't push it McGuire.'

'It's alright for you, you're not over here getting gassed to death.'

'Just get on with it.'

The painting continued as did Mig.

'Listen Wee Man I hate to be the one to break the bad news.'

He put on a look of mock horror and shook his head from side to side.

'Black trainers, nobody wears black trainers anymore.'

Momentarily caught out the Menace looked down at his feet.

'Oops sorry wee man.'

Mig had just dripped emulsion over the shiny new work boots he laughed as the Menace started to reach boiling point.

'Calm down accidents happen.'

Mig was still laughing. Wee Mick was right in there.

'I remember you from school.'

The menace was visibly shaking Wee Mick was grinning and Colin and Mig were all ears.

'You were the one who got caught trying to steel wee Lizzie Armour's knickers off of the washing line.'

There was a resounding laugh. The Phantom Menace real name Robert Grey was harassed frightened embarrassed exposed. He had two options and bursting into tears came a poor second as the paint brush he was holding hit Mick the Mouth in the face with a loud slap. Wee Mick made his best effort at throwing a punch and within seconds they were rolling around the floor. Mig almost pissed himself laughing as Colin and the Supervisor pulled them apart amid flying limbs and loud bravado.

'I'll see you later!'

Shouted young Robert with all the aggression he could muster.

'I'll be there!'

Replied the Mouth who given the audience wished he'd thought up something better.

Ten minute's later emulsion finally washed from his face Mick again rejoined the painting.

'He's getting it after the shift.'

The Daily Record took the two combatants aside and gave serious warnings of imminent Prison sentences he then banished them to separate walls away from Colin and Mig.

'The wife came back then.'

'She came back on Thursday.'

Colin did not feel like going there.

'So how are things with you and Sweet Pamela?'

'Well to be totally honest she's a bit of a live one, known what I mean and the pierced nipples, that was a bit of a turn on. Then she starts referring to me as her man and her kids are calling me uncle Tam. I don't see it lasting much longer besides Wee Linda was a much better shag, she has a bit of meat on her.'

Colin had been brought up to respect women and was less than impressed with the clear minded brutality of Mig's outlook.

'I like Linda, she's alright.'

'If she's really lucky she may still be in with a shout anyway I should worry half the wee slappers that work the west end get their gear from me. Long term relationship, get yourself to fuck, I can have it anytime and extra's.'

The already over sized ego had moved up a couple of gears and though

Colin had no doubt that the Big Mans claims were true for some reason he was not troubled by jealousy, he said nothing.

'Things are on the move, you would not believe the money I've pulled in over the last couple of weeks, it's that much I can't even be arsed counting it. If I had known it was going to be this good our friend Andy Gallagher would have been taken out a whole lot sooner.'

Colin smiled in mock appreciation.

'We will grab a few pints after the shift; I have money to give you.'

Half-ten Colin and Mig are sitting outside having a smoke when they are joined by Mick the Mouth.

'I'm telling you the minute the shifts over, he's getting it.'

Wee Mick had fire in his eye and a fag in his hand they tried hard not to laugh. Meanwhile Robert Grey A.K.A. The Phantom Menace was skulking inside making small talk with the Supervisor and talking to parties unknown on his mobile.

'The wee prick knows better than to come out here!'

The Mouth was showing unusual confidence mostly down to the fact that he had already done over his intended victim when he was in second year.

'What do you think?'

He was brandishing a paint scraper obviously acquired from the paint supplies. Neither Colin nor Mig said anything he slid it back inside his overall and went back in to the unit.

'Get back in here there's walls to be painted.' Shouted the Supervisor.

No one was taking him on and conversation continued in the shape of

Colin voicing his concern.

'The Mouth has a paint scraper the other wee guy will end up all marked up.'

'None of our business and a tenner says Mick will come off

second best anyway we're going to grab a couple after the shift I have money to give you and a favour to ask you.'

Colin's face said it all.

'Calm yourself it's nothing illegal.'

'That'll be a first.'

'I'm going up the town tomorrow their auctioning off ex police vehicles finance re-possessions etc and if I buy something I'll need somebody to bring the Capri back.'

They were suddenly interrupted by the Supervisor who was walking towards them.

'You're here to paint not to sit around smoking.'

They got to their feet and started making their way back in.

'It's the voice of doom.' Said Colin as he got up.

'Don't shoot till you can see the reds of their eyes.'

'I told you already McGuire, don't push it..'

'See that, I knew he missed me last week.'

'I could be missing you permanently a bit like Rigor Mortis.'

After the painting had resumed for a short time the Supervisor disappeared to the toilet.

'As I was saying it's all ex police cars everything from the wee diesel escorts to the traffic pursuit vehicles.'

'I take it your not going there to look at the diesel escorts.'

'Martin tells me they will be auctioning off the big stuff Vauxhall Senators, fastback Rovers etc, but there is also a couple of Cosworth Sierra's up for grabs and I'm into some of that."

Colin wasn't sure about this the Capri it kind of suited Mig but a Sierra Cosworth?

'A Sierra Cosworth is that not a bit over the top for a guy like you?'

'Over the top? For a guy like me; tremendously handsome super stud, feared urban warrior, drug baron extraordinaire.'

Just at that moment the Supervisor re-emerged from the toilet.

'Serious winder upper of community service supervisors, isn't that right.'

The Daily Record pretended not to hear this. Mig though was in full mischief mode the paint tin went over spilling half a gallon of emulsion which quickly started spreading across the floor.

'Oops!'

'Get that cleaned up McGuire!'

'Mig stood there grinning as the paint spread.'

'What with?'

'There's a bucket and mop in the Office.'

Mig pretending to be flustered walked right through the spilled paint right into the Office the only carpeted place in the whole building his size nines spreading perfect white sole prints on the cheap and nasty dark Grey nylon carpet.

'What are you doing?'

Mig looked behind himself in mock horror as an excuse to take a couple of steps back adding all the more to the damage. The supervisor was speechless Mig was not.

'You did ask me to come in here and get the mop.'

'Just get out of there your getting paint everywhere! '

Mig complied with this request making sure to find a fresh bit of carpet on the way out. Unseen by the Supervisor the Mouth having caught the attention of the Menace produced the paint scraper kissed it and slid it back into his overall while grinning evilly. Colin scowled in disapproval.

'None of your business.' Hissed the Mouth.

Meanwhile the supervisor had produced a container of turps and a cloth and was advising Mig to.

'Slap some of that on it.'

More than happy to oblige more than half the contents were poured onto the first foot print.

'McGuire!!!!'

The Daily Record's face looked fit to explode to add to the effect the turps had caused a reaction to the nylon and the carpet started to swell up.

'You asked me to come in here and get the mop. You asked me to put turps on the carpet. I'm only doing what I'm told, honestly there's just no pleasing some folk.'

'If it was left to me you would be in the jail already McGuire.'

'Fuck sake a wee accident a wee drop of spilled paint and you're wanting to jail me for it.'

'Just get it cleaned up.'

He turned to walk away.

'At least the paints not very thick.'

The supervisor turned round and drew Mig a look.

'Jailed for spilling some paint, Hitler could definitely have used a guy like you.'

The Daily Record knew when he was beat and retired to his chair and paper. The rest of the shift dragged in, the air of malice and the promise of imminent violence adding to the usual cheerful atmosphere. As the last few seconds ticked away the Mouth was first at the door a strategy to insure his intended victim did not escape Colin feared for the Menace. Mig on the other hand was looking forwards to some live entertainment the door opened and Mick backed out into the yard he was well ready unfortunately for Mick the Mouth so were the bottom end young team who had been summoned earlier by the intended victim. They were on him in seconds knocking him to the ground and kicking him in all directions. Colin fought off an urge to jump in there was at least a dozen of them Mig pulled him towards the Capri.

'The wee man said it, none of our business.'

As the frenzied violence continued the Supervisor peered out then very quickly closed the door. This was obviously none of his business either.

CHAPTER 19 SAY IT WITH FLOWERS

Colin looked back at the continuing violence now drowned out by the scream of the Capri's tyres.

'I still think we should have done something.'

'What exactly were we going to do? There were at least a dozen of them. Besides it's not as though we owe the wee cunt anything he was the one ready to use the paint scraper.'

His silence confirmed that Colin couldn't really argue with this. Ten minutes later an Ambulance flew past them going in the opposite direction, wailing like a Banshee and flashing like a seventies Disco. Mig slowed down to let it pass.

'That'll be the Wee Man's taxi now.'

The rest of the journey passed in silence. As they entered the pub a six foot space suddenly cleared at the bar. Even Chas Moncrieff who had been boasting about some guy he had been forced to slap lowered it a few decibels. Colin hated himself for liking this and there was Linda service with a smile. He wondered if she would have been just as friendly if she had been there to witness the events of Monday night. A shiver ran through him as he thought about it. The round was procured and after a ten minute twenty pound down spell on the fruit machine it was the usual table.

'Here you go.'

Mig pushed a bulging envelope across the table. Colin quickly pocketed it.

'What's wrong do you not want to count it?'

'What and imply that I don't trust you.'

'Wee Linda's looking pretty tasty I think this could be her lucky day.'

'You think she's going to look at you again after the way that you embarrassed her.'

'Oh yea of little faith.'

Mig swallowed his half and cracked his knuckles.

'A tenner says I can pull her before the night is out.'

'If you don't mind me saying Mig you must be without doubt the most big headed, conceited, self-assured, arrogant bastard that I have ever met.'

'All the qualities that a woman can't resist in a man, right.'

He laughed into his pint.

'I still say there is no way she will look at you again.'

'A tenner on it.'

Colin's annoyance got in the way of his better judgment.

'You're on.'

The topic of conversation, Wee Linda herself approached their table she was carrying a tray of sandwiches.

'These were left over from the pensioner's do yesterday they were wrapped in cling film, so they're still fresh. It would be a shame to throw them out help yourselves.'

Mig looked up at her giving it the charming smile full eye contact and his huskiest tone.

'I'm definitely in to some of that.'

'There's a few gammon left but it's mostly tuna or salmon.'

They helped themselves to a few sandwiches and thanked her.

'Nice sandwiches.'

Commented Colin, unable to take his eyes off of her seductive little rear as she glided over to the next table.

'She just offered me something for nothing and it smells like fish. I think she's trying to tell me something.'

He rubbed his hands together.

'If you like you can give me the tenner just now; it looks like I'm going to be busy later.'

Colin sighed in disbelief his face could not hide his disapproval this had not went unnoticed by gods gift.

'Listen I'm not like you I don't have time for all that romance crap. Say it with flowers, tell me what type of flowers do you buy to say I seriously want into your knickers.'

Just as Colin was contemplating this most intriguing of questions a look of sheer horror spread across his face.

'Fuck sake you look like you've just seen a ghost.'

What he had just seen was a whole lot scarier than a ghost. He lowered his head into his hand exclaiming those immortal words.

'Oh, no!'

Marion had just opened the door looked in and locked on and just as surely as a missile on target was swiftly coming in his direction.

'Well, well Colin Spears imagine finding you in here on a Saturday!'

Sniggers from around the bar added all the more to his embarrassment and gave more fuel to her obvious anger. Mig tried to come to his aid.

'You must be Ma...'

'Was I speaking to you?'

The glare in her eye and snarl in her tone cut him off dead. Colin tried to speak. 'Listen.'

'Listen!!! And what excuse would I be listening to this time.' She paused.

'Well I'm waiting to hear it? No wait don't tell me, you had an accident on the way home. You were just passing by and you fell in.'

Mig started to laugh a mistake immediately put right by the 'turn you to stone' look.

'I only came in for one.' Lied Colin unconvincingly.

'Of course you did!'

'I'll come home when I Finish this one.'

'You either come home right now or don't bother coming home at all!'

An Angel of mercy suddenly appeared in the shape of Linda who had been reluctantly sent out from behind the bar to try and defuse the situation.

'Marion it's been forever since I last seen you, how are you, how are things going, how many month's now?'

'I'm keeping not too bad.'

She glared at Colin. 'But it's not too hard to see how it's going!'

Marion was still angry but Linda's distraction had broken her momentum.

With a look of almost believable concern Mig sprung to his feet and pulled out a chair.

'I'm only saying but if you're pregnant maybe you should take the weight off of your feet.'

'You shouldn't be getting yourself so worked up.'

'I'm getting quite a lot of help with that.'

She looked at Colin, who chose the safest option of saying nothing.

'Mig's right you should sit down even if it's just for a wee while and when Colin finishes that pint I will personally put him out of this pub.'

Reluctantly she sat down, Mig was in there again.

'Can I get you a drink, obviously a soft drink coke orange juice, soda water and lime?'

'Obviously!' Marion replied sarcastically then she reconsidered.

'Alright a soda water and lime. But we're only staying for one.'

Colin was not about to disagree.

'How's Shirley?' Inquired Linda.

'I can't remember the last time I seen her.'

'She's okay but since she married Tony I've hardly seen her.'

'That's no good.'

'She's not the same either; she's got nearly as boring as him.'

Linda was horrified.

'She used to be a scream, remember her hen night?'

'The pub crawl.'

Replied Marion, grinning at the thought of it.

'Remember, remember we went to that club up the town. What was it?'

'Mitzi's' Offered Linda.

Mitzi's that was it. What a night, big Mary was pissed. So we sent Shirley in first to distract the bouncers.'

'Then you and me, we frog marched her in trying to make her look straight.'

Marion was laughing Linda continued.

'The strategic half bottles hidden in the handbags and big Mary strategically hidden in the corner then that guy who tried to chat her up you told him she was deaf and dumb and she was so drunk he believed you.'

Marion was helpless with laughter.

'Just think it would take about four strong men to hold her up these days.'

She was still ending herself when the voice from behind the bar reminded Linda that there were customers to be served.

'I'll have to go, you should come back in for the last hour.'

'It has been a while since I was last out. Are you still at your mother's?'

Linda gave a quick nod while retrieving the empty glasses from the table.

'If I don't see you tonight I'll phone you.'

Colin was touched it was the first time he had seen her really laugh in weeks. Mig by this point had followed Linda to the bar.

'A double southern comfort for me and a soda water and lime for the lady.'

Linda started adding the lime to the soda water.

'I'm impressed; you just saved Colin from getting slaughtered over there.'

The boss asked me to try and calm things down, this pub has seen more than enough trouble recently. If it had been anybody else I would have told him where to go getting in the middle of domestic disputes is not in my job description.'

'I take it you like Colin then.'

'Colin's his own worst enemy, no it was Marion I was there for me and her go back a long way.'

'I still think it was a good thing you did.'

'Don't try and patter me up I heard about Monday night in here.'

'You say Marion is a friend well the guy from Monday night got caught lifting a charity box from the mall. To get off with that he told the police they would find drugs in Colin and Marion's house. The police busted the house and never found anything. Of course the neighbours seen it happen and probably drew their own conclusions. She was so embarrassed that she left him. He was lucky to get her back as for Hodgey he of all people should have known better than to upset somebody I care about.'

Money and drinks changed hands.

'I'm not pattering you up but would you consider going out with me again?'

'Why is the Sweaty Palm knocked up again?'

'No, but she is in the past. Come on we did have good times.'

Mig had just achieved what he had hoped for she had not dismissed the idea right away.

'I can see that you are busy. I'll go away and you can think about it.'

He returned to the table with the glasses, Marion made with polite thanks then all too soon came the awkward silence. Colin struggled to find something positive to say.

'Mig used to go out with Linda.'

Marion looked surprised.

'She's a lovely person more the mug you if you let her get away.'

He put on his best hurt look.

'Don't I know it. I was up there just now trying to ask her back.'

Swallowing his half in one he got to his feet.

'I have to go, I might come back in for the last hour myself and if we are still on for tomorrow you can let me know. If not fair enough.'

CHAPTER 20 PURPLE

Marion gazed out of the window the purple of the Rhododendron was comforting the sky was grey and overcast, the rain had stopped but the wind still blew. Why hadn't she argued harder her common sense had warned her but then her common sense always had been lost on Colin.

The blooms hung low with the weight of the rain. The medication was no longer containing the nightmares and flashbacks. The Saturday night in the pub McGuire insisting on giving them a lift home despite the fact that he had been drinking. Colin and Linda persuading her it would be alright. The sirens, the chase the crash the sound that Linda's head made when it hit the door pillar. The Fire Brigade cutting the car apart the image of Linda on the stretcher like some child's doll with half the head missing. It hadn't taken long she had died before the had gotten her out of the car.

Colin there had not been a scratch on he just started to throw up blood. The doctors had explained he had suffered a ruptured spleen and there were complications. She had prayed with all her might. Oh how she had prayed. On the second day she had lost the baby on the third day she had lost the baby's father.

Outside the wind caused the bushes to play against the bars. She could only vaguely remember the funeral. People had been speaking to her but she had been unable to hear them. McGuire had been there he had come back to the house with the relatives after that she could remember nothing except being in court. The man with the papers saying that; 'The autopsy report on Thomas John McGuire states that of the twenty seven stab wounds and lacerations, cause of death was due to an entry point just under the deceased left shoulder blade where the knife had entered the heart.'

The report also went on to say that the last blow was struck as the victim lay face down on the floor, in fact this blow was struck with such ferocity that the twelve inch blade of the kitchen knife had wedged vertically between the fifth and sixth ribs and was embedded an inch and a half into the floor making it impossible to remove.'

'Marion Tate Spears you shall be taken away for psychiatric evaluation.'

Rain dripped from the blooms.

ABOUT THE AUTHOR

Greig Hepson was born in Johnstone, Renfrewshire in 1960, the youngest of three children, born to May and Thomas Hepson. He grew up in Foxbar on a farm cottage with his parents and older brother and sister. Greig and his wife Davina have three children, a son and two daughters.

Having worked in the furniture industry since he was an apprentice from 1977 – 1986 he then went on to run his own commercial cleaning company for the next nine years. In 1995 he worked as a Community Service Supervisor in the North Ayrshire, East Renfrewshire and Renfrewshire areas.

Greig has always had a great passion for writing, having written countless poems and short stories. As a Community Service Supervisor he found himself in the perfect environment to pick up good material and witty banter for what has now become his third novel. Having started out as a short story 'Serving the Community' has also been adapted by him for film and stage.

In recent years Greig has filmed and directed two of his short stories. His first short film 'The Little People' was shortlisted for the Actor and Writer's Yearbook competition. The more recent 'Alternative Goldie Locks' sees Greig, a trained actor playing the part of a defence lawyer. Both films premiered in the Paisley Arts Centre in 20014.

7156592R00094

Printed in Great Britain
by Amazon.co.uk, Ltd.,
Marston Gate.